Picking Up Pieces

Dearies,
Enjoy these pages"

Sue Frazier

Picking Up Pieces

Susan Frazier

Charleston, SC
www.PalmettoPublishing.com

Picking Up Pieces

Copyright © 2021 by Susan Frazier

All rights reserved.

First Edition

Hardcover ISBN: 978-1-64990-752-3
Paperback ISBN: 978-1-64990-751-6
eBook ISBN: 978-1-64990-753-0

People who encouraged, supported, badgered, and supported my efforts,
especially those who agreed to proofread:

Joann Welter
Diane Duffield
Diane Zalac
Robbie Decker
Sara Lewis
Bonnie Gerda
Margaret Parsons
Larry Grunn
Tina Hille

Corinne Zachos jumped in and helped with photography. Julia Keider consented to
help with technical difficulties and biographical input.

Margaret Parsons spent hours typing the manuscript and allowed her brain to be
picked on ideas. She really was helpful with editing and story line advice.

All the women who pieced the numerous quilts that came to me magically to make
Picking Up Pieces a reality. Most of these quilters I do not know personally, but
their creations are now able to touch hearts and souls and bring comfort and joy.

The reader should know that quilts came to me as if dropped from heaven. I have
fictionalized the story and the quilter and picked up truth when the quilt found me.

Table of Contents

Piecing the Piece

How did this happen? What got me started collecting, saving, finding, finishing quilts and quilt tops? What possessed me to become a quilt rescuer?

Nobody in close family tradition quilted. The one quilt I was solidly familiar with was on my parents' full-sized bed. Usually it was the cover and the bed spread. It was a double wedding ring quilt with a lavender binding. My great grandmother, Peggy Cowan, made it in the 1930's and gave it as their wedding present in 1942. I would lie on that quilt and look for one particular patch that was made up of tiny polka dots. That was my first awareness of a quilt that was a quilt with a history with a known name attached to it.

The second quilt I came to know with a face and a name attached to it was a wedding quilt gifted to us on our marriage in the early 1970's. It was a twin size, predominantly pink, "pinwheel star" made by my husband's grandmother from Parkin, Arkansas. She was a tobacco chewing, God-fearing woman who was poorer than a church mouse. I am here to say that I was a snot about that quilt. It was flimsy material, poor batting, and had, of all things, a mistake in one of the squares. The pinwheel was upside down to the star. I put it in the linen cupboard and sent a "thank-you" note to grandma dutifully.

I tell you now that the quilt came to have a special meaning when in 1975 a neighbor had all the neighbors for brunch at her house. As the morning progressed, another woman became excited at the thought of turning us into a quilt club.

The Bicentennial was coming so it was decided that each of us would make a red, white, and blue quilt with the pattern of our choosing.

Susan Frazier

My first attempt at a quilt patterned after grandma's pinwheels star.

Grandma's scrap quilt

Picking Up Pieces

Prior to this project, I had made the most pitiful, poorly constructed quilt of inferior polyester fabric using the "Sunbonnet Sue" pattern. Not one lady pointed out the obvious deficiencies of this quilt, but I was learning so I dug into the bicentennial project with gusto, I used the pinwheel star pattern of grandma's. In doing so, I found something quite interesting. No quilter that loved the Lord would think of attempting perfection because only God was capable of that. So, women would purposely build something into their quilts that was imperfect. It could be poor stitching in one small area, or a point not meeting perfectly, or a pattern/ block not quite right. Aha! Grandma's upside-down pinwheel star was now explained.

I learned the importance of selecting quality, high-fiber cotton fabrics for longevity. Absolutely no polyester or polyester thread was to be used was just one of the many quilting tips I learned as we gathered monthly in a rotation of our homes.

This activity continued for forty some years. Members came and went, and some moved away. Some passed away. Many never took up quilting, but came to quilt club and crocheted, or just sat quietly and listened and smiled and reveled in the friendly closeness of the couple of hours each month.

In those two hours we learned about quilting, yes, but we learned so much more. We got to know each other personally. We bonded as women with shared experiences. We were wives, mothers, teachers, secretaries, bankers, artists, salesclerks, nurses, and grandmas. The wisdom and shared knowledge is indescribable.

Recipes were shared, valuable advice about any number of issues was shared including: diaper rash, poison ivy remedies, stock solutions, two-year-old temper tantrums, colic causes, teen angst, and myriad other topics.

Memories of days of old, especially in our little corner of the world became cherished nuggets, sometimes told again and again, then remembered much later often causing gales of laughter. One such memory must be shared.

Among us we had two elderly, former elementary teachers of over 40 years who happened to be best friends. Evelyn and Mildred were highly competitive even as friends. Any evening we could be sure to be treated to one, and then another, reciting from memory long poems or lines from plays. They, to our amusement, bickered about small points of fact (or fiction) regarding particular events, names, or dates. One would try to outdo the other or conquer with a louder voice, or longer piece of poetry. Looking at it now, it was amazing to see their ability to remember so many pieces so perfectly. It also was a glimpse into the early childhood classrooms of long ago and the role they played in the social life of the community, and thus in our little quilt club.

As I became quite interested in quilting, I learned of its early colonial beginnings in America. I read any number of novels that were plotted around quilting through the decades starting on the eastern seaboard and moving west. I learned that a quilting effect was used in medieval times as padding under armor and mail, but quilting was used by American colonial women first using rag bits and pieces from work clothes. No longer wearable clothing, not Linsey-Woolsey, but wool or cotton became the basis for patchwork blankets that was picked up and shared throughout the colonies. Creativity, surplus remnants, a loosening of hand to mouth existence emerged. Women started experimenting with original ideas of patterns usually reflecting their surroundings. Plain stars, furrows as in corn rows, squares inside of squares, and any number of patterns thereof, Irish Chain, Granny's Garden, just a plethora of ideas became the essence of quilting that started to pretty up the colonial home.

Economically, quilts moved into the mainstream. A young girl with a hand for quilting became a highly desirable commodity as quilts moved into the dowry agenda. Thirteen quilts providing warmth in many different ways such as the bed, in the cradle, as insulation on walls and floors, as barterable/ tradable goods suddenly zoomed into the bright light of marriage material. Many a covered wagon traveled to the prairie and across the mountains with a trunkful of service-able quilts.

So, this book will take some quilts and provide some stories for your enjoyment, a little piece at a time. Each piece (quilt) with its story will hopefully create a piece of work that tugs at the reader's heart. So many women spent hours and hours snipping, fitting, refitting, imagining, ripping out seams and stitches, saving pennies to buy essentials such as thread, fabric, batting, muslin, slipping down to the gin to stuff gunny sacks with fallen to the ground cotton balls, carding the seeds out of the balls to spread on the backing on the frame, and many other untold tasks to get the quilt to the frame. BUT, think about all the quilts that sat folded on a shelf or in a drawer, never ever seeing use- for all kinds of reasons.

Susan Frazier

What's in a Dream?

We were excited to be going to the "Cousins Picnic" held at the outside of Cleveland farm. We would be staying with a cousin who, as a nurse, had taken responsibility for caring for elderly, single relatives. I say this because as they passed away, she inherited their meager possessions which made staying with her interesting.

While tidying up where my kids had spent the night, I picked up an all-white quilt. As I shook it out, I noticed two spots that were rotted in an otherwise perfectly good, but old, quilt. Inquiring further, I learned that it had belonged to a distant relative who had never married. The spots were explained as unacknowledged results of children wetting the bed. I was instructed to put the rag in the garage.

For some reason, as my arms carried it to the garage, I felt compelled to own this quilt. So, I asked if I could have it. There were raised eyebrows and a question of "Whatever for?" but approval to take the quilt was given. On the way to the farm I was thinking about all our cousins who would be gathering. The thought went back to the quilt folded in the backseat.

"Ginny, whose quilt was that?"

"Oh, let me think. Let's see, Cecil's sister in law, Thea's cousin, Belinda's sister had a sister named Lucille. She was the most accomplished seamstress of any of the girls in that family. She was in demand all over the county. Her specialty was fine, exquisite blouses. They were usually white, had lots of pin tucking and ruffles and lace. Some had beautiful white on white embroidery. She also made beautiful white Christening dresses and baby blanket quilts that family members treasured. She lived with her folks until they died. Then the farm went to her brother. Since women at that time were never allowed to live alone, Tom, her brother was responsible to keep her. Everyone called her Aunt Lucile, the old maid. When she took ill and kept to her bed, she came to live with me. I was trained as a nurse and was happy to have her, such a dear old woman. All year round she had that old quilt on her bed, was fussy about dripping anything on it. Too bad it's got those holes in it now." …. And here, a piece of a story begins.

"I remember sitting one evening with Aunt Lucille, and she got to remembering about a long time ago living on the farm. She clucked a little about sewing up thirteen quilts to bring to her marriage. She put her hand on the white quilt she was covered with and stared at it dreamily. She said, "This was going to be my wedding quilt. Look at how I made those vines run continuously around the whole outside. Everyone liked how I did that. They said so when I was quilting one afternoon. Said it was good luck for long life." She got real quiet then and I thought she fell asleep, but no. She went on to say, "I remember when Ben first looked at me after church one Sunday morning. It was like he just then first noticed me. I had on my best white blouse with all the tucks down the front. I had on a pretty blue floral skirt too. After that day, we saw each other as often as he could get away from his farm work. I thought I had died and gone to heaven. I surely did."

I stretched my arms up toward the ceiling in the early morning light. The window was wide open with no screen, and the wonderfully sweet scent of fresh cut hay wafted up to my room. I leaned on the sill and breathed deeply. Dad waved to me from the barn.

"Lucy! That you? C'mon with ya. There's work to do."

"Okay, okay, Ma, I'm coming."

I snatched the last square of embroidered Calla Lily thinking to bring it down to the dining room where the treadle sewing machine was in the corner. I would add the square to the other three which would make 20 squares for my thirteenth quilt. I touched it fondly, remembering working on it the last several nights by the kerosene lamp in my dormer room. I'd been told it was difficult to use the slightly heavier crewel cord- like white thread on the white grain sacking squares, but I was quite pleased with the results. I planned to embroider curlicue vines around the entire outside of the quilt before I put it in the quilting frame.

"What are you doing in there, Lucy? For heaven's sake, get the eggs, breakfast!"

"Yes, yes! I'm going!"

"Don't forget to get the wash boilers and tubs out of the shed. Boiling water is next up on our list of to-dos."

"Can't Celia get them or the eggs?"

"Okay, she's out messing with those kittens she found out in the ivy. Give her the egg basket."

possibly Lucille's wedding dress

Picking Up Pieces

It was going to be a nice warm sunny day, perfect for wash day in the yard. After breakfast, with dishes done and all the vegetables for noon dinner washed and peeled, I set up the sawhorses. The tripod over the fire pit was still there from last week and the boys had piled the wood for the fire up under the big iron pot. I pumped water into several buckets to fill the pot and lit the fire. I shredded some lye soap into flakes and put them in the copper wash boiler. I filled two more galvanized tubs with cold, clean water. I went into the house to find the first pile of white clothes: cup towels, sheets, underwear, petticoats, pillowcases, napkins, tablecloths and socks and stockings. There was another pile of colorful aprons, dresses and shirts. Beyond that lay the men's overalls, work pants, and work shirts- pretty filthy!

copper wash boiler used on laundry day

I began by stringing the lines from pole to pole and over to the one tree. I got the clothes paddle and the line poles ready at hand and put some of the smaller things into the boiling soapy water. The paddle which really looked like a small boat oar did the job of swirling the glob of clothes and helped to lift them into the rinse water. And so it went all morning. The water had to be changed frequently.

Ma brought out a huge pot of potato water and poured it into a special bucket we used to stiffen some of the items like napkins and blouses and dad's white shirt.

"Okay, honey, we got to get dinner on. The men'll be coming in from haying. Celia! Set the wash basins up over by the shed and put some towels for drying there."

Noon dinner was a raucous affair. Dad, the boys, Uncle Rodney and several hired hands crowded around the table and gobbled pork chops, potatoes, carrots, loaves of freshly baked bread, lemonade, and apple pie.

"Ma, thank ya for another pleasin' meal. We hope to finish the south field and get it in the mow by evening, the Lord willin'. Come on, boys. We're burning daylight."

Ben wiped his mouth and winked at me, turning red. He grabbed his hat off the hook and said, "Much obliged. Love to stay and chin wag, but the hay won't wait."

I smiled at his back which rippled muscularly under his worn plaid shirt. Maybe I could sit next to him in Church on Sunday, but right now there were dishes to be done, water drawn, and the last of the work clothes to wash. By late afternoon with the help of a gentle breeze and a hot sun, the clothes were dry and folded with a pile on the chair by the stove to be ironed tomorrow.

The blackened, wash lye water was poured on the dusty driveway and fire pit ashes, and the gray rinse water was poured on the kitchen garden.

Lucy hurried into the dining room and sat down at the treadle machine and sewed the last block to the row and then sewed the row to the now full-size quilt cover. She hummed as she pumped steadily up and down dreaming about the beauty of this, her finest effort.

Celia interrupted her humming and dreaming by clattering into the room with a kitten in each arm.

"You'd better not let Ma catch those cats in the house!"

"Oh, Lucy, don't tell won't you. I just wanted to see how your quilt was a comin'."

"Just about finished. Won't take me no time to cut six-inch strips, embroider the vines and sew them around the squares."

"Ma gonna give ya some of her white flour sacking she's been saving for petticoats and such?"

"I hope so. I've been saving what I earned from ironing Miss Pritchard's fancy things. She don't want nobody but me doing her ironing. I never scorch nothing."

"Ya, she tells everybody that so's they'll be jealous she's got you."

"Miz Jacobs told me she's got some real nice white cotton thread coming in the store that she'll give me a good price if I'll starch and iron the store's curtains."

"Ya gonna do it?"

"Course! Now get in the kitchen and set the table. Maybe dad will ask Ben to supper."

"Ohhhhh Lucy's sweet on Ben."

"Go on git! Wash your hands after you put those cats outside."

Well, maybe I do take a shine to Ben. We've known each other since we were kids. We hung upside down together in the apple orchard 'til Ma yelled at me about showing my bloomers. Would it be so terrible if we started courtin'?

While I was ironing the next day, Ma said:

"Lucy, I've got all that cotton we picked up at the gin last fall. We should get it carded and ready to set up the quilt frame for your Calla quilt so we can get a Bee a goin'."

I saw those old eyes begin to tear up. She mumbled feebly:

"Guess it was never meant to be. Laws, I stood at the back of the church and saw all my friends and family sittin' in the pews, waitin'. Waitin' and waitin', just like I was. Pa was out front lookin' down the road. Where could he be? Where?

My hands were sweatin' holdin' the bouquet of daisies and asparagus fern. I remembered my trunk by the front door back home, just waitin' to go on Ben's wagon to take us to our new farmhouse.

Suddenly, I heard shouts and heard hooves clattering up to the church. I turned to see Bobby, Ben's older brother, jump off the farm's big old Belgian, Clyde.

Pa tried to stop him from running right up to me, but he pushed him away. "Lucy! Lucy, girl! Ben's dead! Gored and run over by the bull this morning!"

So… that is how I came to own the wedding quilt. And I decided to restore it without knowing one thing about how to do such a thing. I was at an antique shop one day when I spied a table with white flat sheets. I bought one that was soft from use and laundering. I cut out the spoiled areas from the quilt which were two small sections mostly in the quilted areas, not part of the embroidered flower. I then pieced the sheet pieces on one side, used some older quilt batting, and pieced some more sheet onto the back. I then quilted the restored areas. It was a patch job by a know nothing, but it takes a while to find them even when you are looking for them.

I never intended to be a rescuer, of sorts, to lost, unfinished, "hurt" quilts, but that white Calla Lily quilt was the beginning of my becoming a "quilt rescuer." I'd like to think Lucille feels a little dreamy knowing her quilt isn't on the garage floor, absorbing an oil change.

I can only imagine the trouble it saw after Ben's funeral. I can wonder about the twelve other quilts that had been so lovingly packed in the trunk waiting by the front door. What had the years brought to Lucy after all that sorrow?

Lucille's trunk of quilts

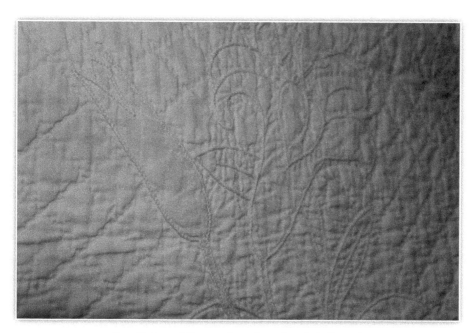

Lucille's wedding quilt embroidered Calla Lily

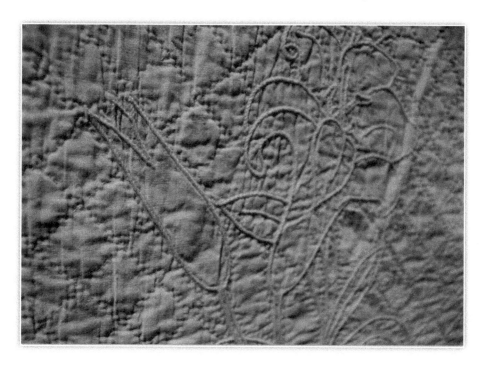

Don't Cha Know?

Okay, I'll say it! Going to school every day is like going barefoot in the middle of winter all uphill both ways. Don't laugh none, neither. Ever since mama up and left taking only her durn dolls with her, life has been more than hard.

Daddy never smiles no more and crabs and grouses at us for every least little thing as he holds together the farm and a job at the electric factory in town. Me, my brother, and my sister have all kinds of chores to do including getting back and forth to school every durn day. My job every morning is to get the water for the cook stove reservoir, the kettle, and the sink pan. I got to haul a pail of water to the chickens too. Billy's got to feed the cows, pigs, and chickens. Beulah feeds the sheep. She takes forever cause she's always kissing her finger and putting it on each of their noses calling them her "sweet things." I got to prod her most every minute to get her in to eat breakfast, pack our one lunch tin with three hard boiled eggs and three slices of the bread Mrs. Murphy bakes and charges daddy ten cents a loaf for. Sometimes I slosh some butter on each piece and wish we hadn't run out of the wild black raspberry jam I made last summer.

When we get to school, I sit right close to the pot-bellied wood stove and wish I could climb in it most days. Beulah and I sleep together in one bed. We have a feather bed mattress, but we put three covers under us (quilt like blankets that have cotton batting but are not made to be pretty. Grandma always tacked/knotted these). We could have five or six quilts on top of us. Even so during the winter when the wind blows, snow sifts in around the window and we wake up with a dusting of snow across the bed. Don't cha know we hop out of bed and run down to the kitchen cook stove to get washed and dressed.

pot belly stove similar to schoolhouse stoves

I will say I am quick to get my sums done and my states and capitals all remembered cause then I can go over in the corner with two or three of the younger ones and read to them or listen to them read to me. We only go to school from late November through early March 'cause we're needed at home to help on the farm.

Well, guess what? Today Miss Abel told the whole class we are going to get started on our school project. She was so delighted to show us a bag of scrap fabric that a big ol' church in Detroit had sent her aunt who had no use for it. Well, Miss Abel says she knows what to do with it. We are to make a quilt. We? Yes, all fourteen of us are going to cut and piece and quilt, not tack a quilt.

So, it began. In the morning we did our learning, and in the afternoon, we sorted fabric and began to cut. Miss Abel showed us all kinds of cuts and angles and said it was close to doing Geometry. I guess I'll tell you that this bag of pieces was the strangest fabric I ever did see. Homer and Grubs guffawed when they saw it and pretty much said it was woman's work. They weren't having none of it. Miss Abel had to put a stern face on and tell them what an important skill it is to thread needles, cut around a pattern, sew straight stitches. Everyone needed to be able to do that. I got to tell you though; she hit home when she told them that fabric came from men's underwear and pajama scrap material. Manly stuff, that! They laughed and laughed and snorted about who wears any pajamas or underwear!

I got my hands on some red paisley bits and you know what, don't cha know I cut them bits into hearts. I pieced placed them on this striped fabric. It got so I hurried through the mornings and even started to get to school ahead of all the others. I stoked the ashes in the stove, threw some kindling in, and pretty soon had a real nice fire going where I could sit right next to and get to my piecing.

Wish I could tell you how happily that year turned out. Daddy died; don't you know? Uncle Tom and Aunt Rita said they'd take Billy because they could use him on the farm. Mama still wasn't having anything to do with us. She was off in the city managing her doll store. She made outfits, sewed wigs and fashioned shoes for rich folks' girls' doll babies. So, a neighbor, the Grovers, agreed to take Beulah and me. They had two grown sons.

Miss Abel made a surprise announcement in early March. She was getting married. After that interest in the quilt just kinda faded away. It was folded on the shelf. Her last day after everyone had run out of the schoolhouse, she asked me to stay a moment.

"Helen, I have something for you." She gave me a brown paper wrapped package. "You should have this. You put the most work into it and were long enthusiastic. You'll see that it gets finished somehow. I know you will."

Well, don't you know she gave me that durn underwear/ pajama quilt top!

I hauled it home and Mrs. Grover just shook her head and said it was the oddest, ugliest top she'd ever laid eyes on. I put it on my closet shelf....

... It was Thursday evening at Zion Lutheran Church and the ladies were setting up long rows of tables in the church hall.

"Girls, we'll put boxes under the tables to make it easier to break down the sale on Saturday afternoon."

Alice had done this for several years each spring and fall for the rummage sale, a really good fundraiser for the church.

"This whole table will be for children's clothes with any toys at the very end."

Rana Lynn asked if we could put the housewares and the miscellaneous over by the exit and was pleased to get an okay. Part of one row of tables was labeled for fabric remnants, bed linens, and towels for work room and car washing needs.

Donations started flowing in and the women busied themselves organizing in readiness to open in the morning. Bonnie hauled her black garbage bags in already presorted for placement. She had spent several months over the winter cleaning out her mother's house. The rummage sale was a perfect outlet for a ton of useful things. The last bag had fabrics, sheets and towels. Oh, and there was an old pieced quilt top. All went on the table neatly folded.

"Okay, ladies let's roll! Today most clothing is twenty-five cents per piece. Coats are one dollar. Men's suits are five dollars. There is a dollar table for miscellaneous. Tomorrow a grocery bag will go for five dollars out the door."

George chimed in with:

"And hopefully it will all go so I don't have to make a trip to the Salvation Army."

Bonnie hustled and was pleased to see a crowd rummaging away at the tables. Alice whispered furtively, "Oh look, there's that woman who comes every time and takes all the jewelry we have. Wonder what she does with it."

"Why I know!" reported Bonnie. "She makes her own jewelry out of recycled beads, chains, and jewelry parts and sells them at craft shows."

"Oh yes! There is another woman who'll come in tomorrow and load up grocery bags with the fabrics. She makes quilts for the homeless."

Bonnie looked over at the table and saw a woman pick up the quilt top and immediately put it back down. She heard her comment about how ugly it was which made Jane go over and look at it more closely. Another woman stood next to her and squinted at it.

"Looks like men's pajamas and underwear material was used to make that. Who would ever put paisley hearts on that?"

Saturday afternoon came, and I showed up for clean-up committee duties. We began putting leftover clothing in the boxes from under the tables. Lots of polyester shirts and pants were left unwanted. There was hardly anything left on the linen and towel table except this wadded-up piece. I put it in the box, but Bonnie stopped me saying:

"You know… that was at my mom's house. It was in an old trunk with scraps of red paisley. It needs washing. It really does, but how many quilts have you ever seen made out of pajama and underwear material? Why don't you take it! You could do something with it, Sue. Don't you belong to a quilt club? It will just get shredded to make industrial rags."

So, I took the quilt top home after asking Bonnie her mother's name.

"It was Helen. She was just the sweetest lady ever. We loved to hear her stories, especially after she went to live with Grovers. Mrs. Grover so loved my mom, never having a girl of her own. She was partial to Helen. Said she was such a strong, capable little thing, so quiet but a wonderful observer and listener."

And don't cha know I finished the underwear/ pajama quilt with a deep red and black backing, machine quilted in hearts and curlicues and bound in the same fabric. Many who have seen it, admire its uniqueness and declare it quite collectable. It is not so very odd or ugly, "Don't cha know!"

Picking Up Pieces

Until this quilt came to me, I had no awareness of pajama or underwear fabrics. But of course, it was a necessity so why, wouldn't there be remnants or scraps perfectly useful for quilting.

Since then, three quilts have found their way to me. One was more of a lap quilt or baby quilt. The other two were part of four quilts that were found in a large wooden box in a chicken coop. They were serviceable, necessary quilts that were well-used but with very few holes. They both, actually, all three had the small striped blue fabric found in most men's pajamas from 1890-1910. In fact, when going through a relative's chest of drawers, when clearing out the house, there it was! A pair of men's pajamas! In the traditional small striped blue material with drawstring bottoms. And there's more! There too, were boxer drawers made from the small dotted, light grey/ white material.

finished rummage sale find

Aloha

June 1893-

Extra! Extra! Read all about it!
U.S. loves Hawaii!
Cleveland shakes his finger!
Queen Liliuokalani overthrown!

Hattie looked down on the sidewalk from the open window and listened to the newsboy hawk papers. Pastor Frampton had just visited and talked about the Franks sending a letter to him from LaHaina. Our church sent them with several barrels of clothing and goods to the islands as missionaries. They thrilled us with descriptions of blue skies, sunflowers, something they ate called Poi, and lots of other interesting details about life in Hawaii, including curious habits of the native Hawaiians.

Americans couldn't get enough of the news from Hawaii. They clamored for stories about the palace in Honolulu, or the black sand beaches. News of an active volcano and long dead Diamondhead were digested and discussed and speculated about around the dinner table.

Dad had invested in sugar and was worried about how annexation would affect the world trade markets. What if tariffs were lifted or increased? The natives weren't too happy about foreigners taking over their land and bossing them around. In fact, unrest had bordered on riots! Oh, it was all so deliciously exotic.

Hattie patted her ring curls, still tight from the rags rolling them tight overnight. She pinched her cheeks, stepped into her new ballerina slippers and flounced down the stairs, pretending she was the queen of Leilani palace.

It came to her then that wouldn't it be grand to have an afternoon party for some of the ladies she socialized with, mostly through sewing circle, and have a Hawaiian theme. Why, they could have a tropical punch in mom's new cut glass bowl with matching cups. She bet Cook could make a fruit salad, even if they didn't have any pineapples or coconuts.

Hattie helped herself to eggs, bacon, and scones from the sideboard. As she sat down, mother joined her, beautifully dressed.

"Are you going out this morning, mother?"

"Yes, dear, I'm planning on visiting Lottie Frampton to plan for the Ladies Tea in May."

"Oh! Wonderful! I was hoping to write Mr. and Mrs. Franks in Hawaii and ask them some questions. Could you get their address for me?"

"Whatever for!?"

"I just think it's so exotic. I'd love to know more, plus I was thinking of having a luncheon with our sewing group and theme it Hawaiian. Don't you think that would be fun?"

Days later Hattie sat down to start to write a letter which read as follows:

Dear Mrs. Franks,

I hope this letter finds you well and enjoying what I am told is warm and sunny every day, even when it rains.

It has been humid and hot here. In church on Sunday many hand fans were overworked. Luckily, Reverend Franks told us quite an interesting story that the Catholic priest from St. Joseph's told him at lunch the other day. I'll share it with you as it reminded me of the work you are doing there in LaHaina.

Saint Fiacre was born in Ireland in the 600's. He and several other monks were sent to Europe to spread God's word. Fiacre wished to be a hermit and petitioned the Bishop of Paris to have a place of his own deep in the forest where he could lead a prayerful, contemplative life. He cleaned a space, built a small chapel to Our Lady and began a small garden which very quickly grew larger. Hunters were greeted and welcomed and enjoyed a place of plenty, meaningful preaching, and wondrous healing using herbs and wildflowers. Flocks of humans came in such numbers that Fiacre had to build a structure for the visitors and enlarge his gardens to the point of having to ask the Bishop for more land.

The Bishop thought about it and said, "Fiacre, you may have as much land as you can enclose with your spade in one day."

Daunted, Fiacre calculated what his needs would be and fretted at the task with his shovels he went into his humble chapel and prayed fervently.

Picking Up Pieces

Unbeknownst to him, a jealous woman from the village nearby who had been the healing woman and had advised peasants of their ailments was not happy with his presence. She was hiding in the brush and watched. The next morning, Fiacre's prayers were answered. A large tract of land was enclosed by the spade. The woman went to the Bishop and accused Fiacre of witchery, but the Bishop was so taken by the event that he declared it a miracle and cited Fiacre a Saint. Angered by the woman's charges he called HER the witch and proclaimed Fiacre in charge of a man only monastery. Rumor had it that any woman who entered would go blind or mad.

This place became a Benedictine Prior and in the simple garden that grew and grew many wonders of healing occurred. Sometime in the 1600's Fiacre's remains were moved to the Cathedral at Meaux where they rest today, and St. Fiacre continues to be considered the patron of gardens and healers.

As I left church, I couldn't help but notice the beauty of flowers and gardens and tended lawns and again thought of you and the flowers and shrubs that surround your house.

I was wondering if you could tell me if the Hawaiian women do any quilting or needle work. I am hoping to drum up a little interest in your mission work by hosting a Hawaiian themed sewing day with traditional food for lunch. I need your help to let me know what that might be.

Thank you for any help or advice you may have for me. Thank you and Mr. Franks for serving the Lord.

Yours Truly,

Hattie

Weeks went by and Hattie and her friends were busy going for walks in the park, learning the art of flower arranging and chair coning, and most of all hoping for a beau. Robert Gravely had most recently asked Hattie and her mother to go for a carriage ride to his grandparents' cottage on the lake. All had been arranged and a lovely afternoon was spent chatting about the family farm in Michigan. Hattie learned that Robert's interest was in agriculture and that he hoped to one day oversee a dairy herd of over 100 cows. Hattie exclaimed:

"Oh my goodness! How could you ever take care of that many animals?"

"Actually, Hattie, it is a science and a great deal of planning, hard work, good hired help, and a cooperative married couple spirit all come together for success," replied Robert's grandfather looking knowingly at his wife.

Robert looked sideways with a winsome smile at Hattie that made her heart flutter.

They returned as dusk was setting in and Hattie's mom thanked Robert for the dry, safe, carriage ride and invited him for Sunday dinner which brought another smile to him.

Hattie skipped up the stairs into the foyer and saw an envelope posted from Hawaii addressed to her. She snatched it and ran up to her room.

Upon opening it, she read:

My Dear Hattie,

I received your lovely note and was delighted by your story about that Fiacre fellow. I shared it with Mr. Franks who thought he might use it one Sunday himself. So, thank you ever so much.

I know you would love living here. Whaling ships can be seen along with big Schooners carrying cargo in the LaHaina harbor. Lovely perfumed by Plumeria and orchid breezes float through our open-year-round windows.

We have papaya, mangos, and some bananas at every meal. Roasted meats are frequently smothered in palm leaves and slowly simmered over an open fire. I know you have heard of

Poi which has the consistency of pudding. It is made from Taro root which has been pounded into mush. Babes love it and the Hawaiian people slurp it up with their fingers. I also imagine you have had some coconuts by now. There's always fish to eat-not the Cod you are used to, but Mahi-Mahi and Dolphin. Very different getting used to.

I did some investigating about quilts. Several women in my Bible study group listened to my inquiry but didn't offer any ideas; however, one quite elderly lady saw me after group and invited me for a home visit the next day.

Leilani welcomed me into her simple but lovely home. It was very comfortable feeling. Over tea, she had her granddaughter bring several blankets to where we were sitting.

"Eleanor, you must understand about our Hawaiian tradition. Our quilts are not made for warmth or display. Each pattern is closely guarded so it won't be copied. They are works of art- an expression of the maker. Each of us has one special quilt that contains our "mana," our spirit which is to be burned when we die. These quilts, really all of our quilts are to be treasured. They hold in their stitches and patterns the love, feelings, and our ancestors' stories. We check weekly for mildew, wear from creases, and damage from chewing varmints. We do not favor many colors in out quilts. If you look at those you will mostly see only two colors. The pattern is one and the background is one."

Hattie, I wish there was a way to picture these quilts for you. Many of them are appliqued with the tiniest of hidden stitches, truly works of art they are.

I hope this helps you decide whether to create a Hawaiian type quilt or not.

When next I hear from you, I will be in Honolulu. We are going to help establish another mission church near the now quiet volcano, Diamondhead.

Sincerely,

Eleanor Franks

Mrs. Gravely! Mrs. Gravely! Yoo-hoo, Mrs. Gravely!

Hattie started! For a minute she had to get her bearings. She'd been lost in that batch of old letters- over twenty years old already. She was Hattie Gravely now, wife of Robert Gravely, owner of 250 acres in Livingston County, Michigan. She went to the screen door to greet Gladys MacKenzee.

"Hi Gladys, sorry about keeping you here at the door."

"Well, Hattie, I was just a little worried until I seen you coming down the stairs."

"I was up in the storage room trying to arrange all that junk. I just found a trunk that I brought from home years and years ago. Who knows what I've yet to find!"

It was two hours later that Gladys was walking down the lane to her house. It appeared she was feeling the lonesome and had come a callin'. Robert would be coming in for midday lunch. Hattie had it all set since early this morning. She didn't know if he'd bring any men with him.

Gladys had told her that Schmiegel's barn had burned to the ground the other night. The constable said maybe vagrants had set it. Luckily, it was empty.

She and Robert had been lucky as many stopped and asked for directions or a bite to eat or a night stay in the dairy barn. They were never turned away so that might have helped with no theft or destruction. God is great.

She looked up from setting the table to see Robert coming in the door. While he was humming and washing up, Hattie commented that he had brought no hired men for lunch. He turned to her and said:

"I just wanted some you and me time today. I am glad Gladys went on down the road."

As he was finishing up his blueberry pie, he put his hand over Hattie's and said:

"Thank you, Hon. I'm proud that you're my wife. I know it's been hard sometimes, especially to be away from your folks. I just love that you love me. I do want to talk a bit about this farm and what might be comin'. You know I don't hold with no banks. I don't like nobody else knowin' my business. I got an uneasy feeling that somethin' bad's comin'. So, I want you to know what I been doin'. Every time I get some cash, I go down in the basement to the far north wall. Long time ago when I came here for summers, I pulled some stones away and had a little treasure spot. I put arrowheads that I found in there. Since then, I've been fillin' up your canning jars with cash. There must be eleven or twelve there now. I, and now you, know about this. When hard times come, we'll be okay with God's help."

Hattie bit her bottom lip before she said, "Robert, should Heather and Bill know too?"

"Absolutely not! They left this farm as soon as they could get on the train. No way!"

With that he got up, put on his hat, gave Hattie a hug and went to his barn and his cows and his prayers.

Years and years later...

"I've hired an auction company so there will be a sale here in late June. We will auction the land in parcels according to the surveyor. The barns, the house, and 20 acres will go as one parcel. You can expect we will have a 'Honey Wagon.' You can sort all your household stuff and portion it in boxes as you wish."

Hattie sat at the table and dabbed at tears. It was so hard to believe. And still the children hadn't come. Neither one of them had married, no grandchildren, no one to leave family mementos. Worse than sad. All those quilts made, and all those still to finish and quilt, even the Hawaiian one from long ago Baltimore before Hattie was married. At least it had seen top finishing. Hattie remembered embroidering 1896 in the lower corner before she folded it and put it in the fabric box that went in the sewing trunk. But now... now what?

Sue's husband came in from work and announced that there were auction signs up at the farm down the road for Friday and Saturday.

"I've never been to a farm auction," Sue said.

"Well, Friday's livestock, so I guess if you wanted to go, Saturday be your day."

Midmorning, Sue walked down to the farm with some cash in her pocket. There were several rows of farm wagons full of boxes and bins. Some had tools and screws and nuts and bolts. One wagon was all household stuff. Sue walked along and peered into several boxes and found one that had kitchen and miscellaneous hodge-podge stuff. Of all the boxes this one had some things Sue could use in the kids' playhouse. The auctioneer was close and starting on this wagon. He came to her chosen box and said:

"Okay, who'll give me 2 dollars? Two dollars, two dollars..."

Sue raised her hand at two dollars.

"Two dollars once, twice, SOLD for two dollars!"

A thrill went through Sue. Her first buy at an auction. She picked up the box, took the bid slip and went to the pay table then walked on home.

When she arrived, no one was home. She put the box on the kitchen table and started unloading her treasures. It didn't take long, and all the stuff was spread out. There was a flour sifter, a metal funnel, some old sewing scissors, a packet of needles, a pair of clip on earrings, some plastic cups and saucers- good for the playhouse. Down to newspaper at the bottom of the box. Sue wanted to see the date on the newspaper and picked it up.

What?!

Oh my gosh!

There under the paper was something like a cloth folded up.

Sue picked it up and it fell out of its folds.

Pale yellow, very simple, patches were expertly appliqued on very soft white fabric. Looking closer, Sue surmised the white fabric could be flour or sugar sacking. Shaking it out, Sue saw on the one corner the numbers 1896 satin stitched in the corner. The patches were reminiscent of Hawaiian floral patterns Sue had seen when visiting Honolulu.

The Hawaiian quilt top was the delight of "Show and Tell" at quilt club that month.

Donna marveled at how extraordinary the condition was.

"My goodness! It isn't yellowed or faded or frayed. What a find! You going to quilt it?"

Sue had thought on this and had already decided to take it to Rhonda Loy. Rhonda was amazed at the condition and looked it over with an expert eye.

"I think because of the age that we should stipple this. It will be strong and long lived. A muslin backing and muslin binding would be most appropriate."

Done!

Aloha!

Ain't that Something!

"**M**artha! Maaarrthaa! Where are you? Get yourself down here and help me with these chairs. There's only ten of them and we need thirteen. The Wilsons are bringing three and the Delaneys are bringing three more. Dad dropped the quilting frame down from the ceiling. I cleared off the sideboard and put out what thread we have and some needles. More will come with the girls. Martha! Did you hear me?"

"Oh Ma! Calm down, will you! Nobody's gonna be here for another hour and then they'll help if we aren't ready. You know they do. They like to come to be here. We got the biggest room for quiltin' don't we?"

"Shush! Them windows clean? Any dust on those chairs? Did you sweep the floor good?"

"Ma, we did all this yesterday. Quit fussin'!"

"Oh my gosh! Martha! Did you lime the outhouse? Did you put the Sears catalog out? Glad the lilacs are in bloom. It'll smell real swell. Take the broom out there and go over the walls and floor once more. Spiders might of marched in overnight."

"All right, okay, yes ma'am!"

"Yoo Hoo! Yoo Hoo! Howdy girls! I came early and brought my chairs. Tillie and Henri are totin' them in. Thought we'd get here a little early and help ya get the muslin backing on the frame. I'll quick baste it all around so we can put the cotton we carded on top of that. Lordy! I can't wait to see all them rings we got all sewn together. Just wonderful that Landis Let us take the truck, old as it is. Really hard to crank to get it to turn over."

"Wonder how much we are going to bring in! Let me think now, there's 24 squares and each of us is gonna try to get 25 cents a name and try to get at least 16 names to embroider in a circle on a square, so that's 4 dollars a square, so that's a total of $96 for our fundraiser! Yippee skippee!! Won't it be fine?!"

Just then, Ethel peeked through the open window.

"Lookee here! I got two ladder back chairs with me. Girls, come and shore them up to the table. Here's two cushions. Butts will be sore by this afternoon! Yes, sirree!"

"Lawd, Lawd, Thelma! You're all red in the face. Sit yourself down and catch your breath. You wanna glass of water?"

"I'm fine, just fine! So happy to get out of the house. The wagon ride over was a treat even if it was bumpy. Spring smells so divine. Even the mud and the horse sweatin' didn't wrinkle my nose.

Dottie Mae was coming through the backdoor with a basket on her arm. She marched right over to the table and flipped back some cup towels to see what was for eats.

"Oh, I just love ham, potato, asparagus and cheese casserole. Yumcious scrumptious! I made my poppyseed cake with my mom's heavenly frosting. Yes, siree, yumcious, scrumptious!"

Just then Freda popped in carrying a stuffed pillowcase. It had been her job to sew all the squares together. Several women had speculated on how she would do it. Would she frame each one? Would she just outline the sewn together squares in a solid color? Would she just leave the squares of muslin and embroidered names in a circle on the muslin with no border at all?

Martha moved over to Tillie and Henri who were putting out spools of thread and packets of needles.

"Think they'll let us do any quiltin' today?"

"Why, Henrietta Wilson! You know blame well that you ain't even put together that doll blanket yet- much less quilted it! You just stand there and start threadin' needles and put any quiltin' foolishness right out of your head."

Tillie giggled and ducked her head as she reached for a spool of white thread and said:

"Yup, same as I told her this morning- No way!"

Out of the corner of her eye, Martha caught sight of Leona tippy toeing in from the kitchen.

"Hey, Lee!"

Leona crunched her shoulders and put the tip of her braid in her mouth but didn't say anything.

Tillie elbowed Martha and whispered:

"She can't even thread a needle! All she's going to do is hide under the table and stare at the shoes and feet!"

"Shhh, she'll hear you! Be quiet!"

"Ma says she ain't right in the head. Slow, ya know? She can't carry on a conversation a'tal. I can't even figure out what to say to her."

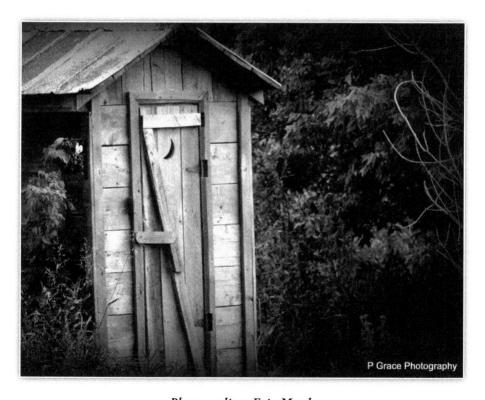

Photo credit to Erin Mead.

Josey pushed in just then and started right in about how she heard her ma and dad talkin' about a rich couple over in Hickory Corners whose son had gone missing eight months ago. They figured he'd walked too close to the swamp and an alligator got him!

"Oh, Josey, you're always coming up with some wild story that we're supposed to think is true cuz you say you heard your folks talking about it!"

"Well, I'm telling you this is true. It got wrote up in the paper even cuz somebody saw a young boy with a Tinker and thought he looked like the Reynolds boy."

"So?"

"Well, the sheriff looked into it, and the Tinker admitted to kidnapping him! So there! Ain't that something!"

By the time the four girls had sixteen needles threaded, they looked up to see Freda and Thelma had the muslin stretched by basting to the quilt frame and were pulling cotton wads out of an old pillow case and putting them into place on the muslin, ever so occasionally, picking a seed out Other women had arrived with a dish to pass and their own little sewing baskets. Opal had one that was so sweet. It was octagon in shape and had a cover woven with sweet grass. She said her auntie had it given to her by her grandpa who bought it from a Cherokee squaw. In it she had a thimble, some needles, and some beautiful scissors shaped like a bird that her mama gave her when she was twelve. She never let nobody use them at the frame, only her.

Freda nodded to Cecil, president of the K.E.E. Sewing Club, to begin the Bee.

"Ladies, I call to order the K.E.E. Sewing Club, this fifteenth day of May, 1941. Let us bow our heads in prayer. Our Father, who art in Heaven…"

As the prayer ended there were murmurs of excited anticipation to see the finished top which Freda held in a pillowcase in front of her. Freda began:

"Ladies we decided to raise some money by each of us collecting sixteen signature names of people who donated twenty-five cents to have their names embroidered on a muslin square to be part of a twin size quilt, which would be raffled off to the winner of 384 entries. We have twenty-four squares and have collected $96."

Applause sounded around the frame. "You appointed me to sew up the squares to make the quilt top. I'll show you now what I have done." As she unfolded the top, she said, "I framed each square in yellow. I then framed the yellow with a muslin border. All of the names you embroidered, I told you to separate with a black embroidered line shooting from a circle centered in the muslin square which has your name in the very center. So here it is."

Appreciative gasps were heard in the room.

"As you can see, I took the liberty of penciling in the quilting pattern to be used in the frame and the border. We will stitch the circle with the black rays out to the yellow frame. While we quilt, we can talk about what color binding to use, how are we going to date and call for the raffle, and who or what our fundraiser money will go to. Any questions or comments?"

Cecil responded and said, "Thank you, Freda so very much. I hope we can quilt this up today. I urge all of you to pay attention to your stitches. We are aiming for nine stitches to an inch. I know some of you can get fourteen, but nine is our goal. The girls will keep this top stretched over the cotton and backing and get it basted down."

The women all got busy and quickly were ready to baste.

By the sideboard, Joesy conspiratorially began with, "My grandma was telling me about a family over Lorain County way who if they didn't have any bad luck, they wouldn't have any luck at all. As she said it started when their farm was hit by a tornado a while ago. They lost a thousand chickens- never found a one! Their barn blew over and killed eight beef cows and twelve pigs with twenty-three piglets. She said she saw a piece of straw driven like a nail into a pole in the yard. And to top it all, the house they were sleeping in when the storm came through, was knocked clear off its foundation! Ain't that something!"

Marta and Lillie rolled their eyes at each other while Joesy threaded up another needle.

At the frame, the girls set to quilting and were quiet for a while. Then Amelia shyly spoke.

"I wonder if you would like to hear a poem I found in the Ladies Home Companion. I memorized it just for fun."

Nods approval and yes murmurs spurred Amelia to say:

Susan Frazier

The Quiltmaker

By Dora Stockman
Bits of calico, green and blue
Yellow and red and many a hue
Scraps of aprons, dresses and shirts
Left to the ragbag's neglected deserts.
Garments worn for work a day
Clothes for Sunday,
Clothes for play
Cut to a pattern and sewn together
Busy hands work for any weather
Set together in the strips and blocks
In lonely hours
When the clock tick-tocks,
Quilted in patterns quaint and old
Stitched with memories yellow and gold
Every piece has a story to tell
Tales of laughter and tears that well,
Tales of life with its patterns and seams
Tales of hopes and cherished dreams
Pieced and stitched and quilted together
Busy hands work for any weather.

Birthia smiled and asked if Amelia would recite it once more. All the women around the frame voiced approval.

She thought about how many times her mom had tried to teach her to use a needle and thread. How many times they had cut patches for a doll quilt only to have her mom actually sew it together and then quilt it. No, she would never have a stock of quilts to take to a marriage. She didn't even know nobody to marry. She had wanted to give her mom 25 cents to embroider her name into the quilt above her head, but she only had the two Indian head pennies she found in the dirt by the general store. She couldn't even win the quilt, let alone stitch it.

Leona, under the frame, secreted from the women and staring at their knees and shoes, nodded delightedly to hear it again. She never would be able to create a patchwork quilt. It was just beyond her how anybody could make all those pieces come together so beautifully. She slipped the end of her braid into her mouth and twirled it with her tongue while she listened to Amelia's distant voice.

Just then Cecil declared a break for lunch.

Henri, Marta, Tillie and Joesy took their full bandanas out under the oak tree and sat down to eat. No sooner had they crossed their legs, Indian style, than Joesy said:

"My uncle Joe, who is the postmaster, was telling us kids about the Pony Express at Sunday table. I remember everything he said. He said that in St. Joseph, Missouri on April 3, 1860, a mail pouch with 49 letters, 5 telegrams, and some miscellaneous papers left for San Francisco, California.

Did you know that a fresh horse was needed every ten-fifteen miles? A fresh rider was needed every seventy-five to one-hundred miles. Seventy- five horses were needed one way, and they moved at about ten miles an hour. Well, Uncle Joe said that on April 9th at 6:45 p.m. the rider arrived in Salt Lake City, Utah, then Carson City, Nevada saw a rider at 2:30 p.m. on April 12th! And guess what! On April 14, 1860- 11 days from start to finish- the mail pouch was delivered in San Francisco! Ain't that something?"

The girls were quiet for a minute until Tillie asked, "Whatever happened to the Pony Express?"

"Well, don't you know? The Telegraph happened!"

Dottie Mae called out the back door, "Girls! Get in here and look after these kids! Get 'em cleaned up and down for naps. Then, pick up the kitchen and do the dishes. C'mon now! No dilly-dallying!"

Marta whispered, "Maybe we can lollygag!"

The girls giggled all the way to the back-door water pump to wash up again. They pumped a ready bucket full to put on the stove to boil for washing dishes.

The ladies bumped and scraped chairs back at the frame when Freda said, "Ready to roll? Are we all square? Remember tight now. Roll! Just look! Just see how much we got done this morning. Good job, Ladies. We will be done by early afternoon, won't we?!"

Talk commenced right after Nelly gave thanks to the Lord for bountiful food, friendship, and good weather.

Myrtle remarked about Pauline's oatmeal cookies that she had brought to share and asked if she would be willing to share her recipe. Pauline turned red and said:

"Tweren't nothing. It was my grandma's. Always use it to make a mess for the boys. Got it right here in my head. I like to double it if I got all the fixins."

Freda said maybe the girls could copy it down for anybody that might want it.

Pauline's Oatmeal Cookies

400*
8-12 minutes
Grease Sheet

Cream:	Add: 2 cups flour
1 cup butter	2 cups oatmeal
¾ cup white sugar	1 tsp. Cinnamon
2 eggs	1 tsp. Salt
2 tsp. vanilla	1 tsp. Soda
	1 tsp. Hot water
	1 cup raisins/ nuts

The afternoon passed quickly and Marise, Leona's mom, asked how they were going to handle the raffle.

Several suggestions were offered. Dorothy wondered if they should offer it for more tickets. Coralene was upset because that would take away from those who paid for the stitched name to possibly win it. It was decided to display it at the Fourth of July Picnic with the drawing at noon. Marise volunteered to bind it and bring it to the picnic. All agreed.

A closing prayer followed, and the ladies packed up and headed for home, the quilt neatly rolled in an old pillowcase with leftover fabric to make the binding tucked in Marise's tote basket, which Leona carried proudly to the wagon.

Fourth of July dawned gloriously and promised to be a warm one. Marise barked orders to her husband, Tom, and Leona. She fried chicken, made coleslaw and fresh baked rolls were packed around a big jug of lemonade in the wicker basket. Straw was loose in the wagon bed.

When they got to the town square there was a hubbub of noise and a squash of people. Tom and Marise Walker hurried to find a shaded spot to spread their tarp. Leona stayed a while in the wagon sucking on her braid.

Cecil and Freda and several other girls hurried over and said they'd stretched a rope between two trees to hang the quilt. Marise called to Leona to bring the quilt right quick.

Leona wasn't to be found. She had crawled under the wagon and tried to hide herself.

She was all flustered, sweaty, and feeling all nervous at what she'd done. Really couldn't believe she'd done such a thing. She looked up at the bottom of the wagon bed and pushed at the pillowcase shoved between the flat of the wagon bed and a cross beam above the axle.

Tom and Harold came looking for her. They leaned against the wagon and had a swig of last year's cider from the well of the wagon.

"Where in Tarnation is that girl?"

"Beats me! There's no tellin' what's got in her head."

They called some more and stomped off. Leona cringed, crawled out, and walked toward the square, shoulders hunched.

Joesy, Tillie, Gertie, and Marta came running up to her and said everybody was looking for her. What was she doing? She just shrugged her shoulders and walked even slower and stopped when her mother spied her.

"Leona, where's the quilt? I told you to bring it. Now, where is it?"

"I don't know, mama."

"What do you mean you don't know? I told you to put it in the wagon. Where is it, girl?"

"Mama, I don't know. I just don't know!"

"I told you to put it in the wagon. I put it in your hands. Did you do that?"

"Yes."

"Well, it's not there or here. Where is it?"

Dottie Mae said, "Yes, child, where is it?"

Leona was sucking furiously on her left braid. It was soaking wet. Her father yanked it out of her fingers and said, "Enough, Leona! Tell us where the quilt is!"

Joesy piped up just then and said, "Someone should ride back down the road and see if it somehow fell out."

"That's a good idea," Henri spouted.

Harold was already in the saddle and on his way.

"Marise, what's going on?" Freda asked gently, but she was clearly disturbed about the turn of events, as were the sewing club ladies. The raffle was due to happen in fifteen minutes.

Nelly thought a silent moment of prayer was in order. Pastor Stone nodded in agreement. Time passed and Harold returned, his horse in a sweat with no quilt to be seen.

By late afternoon, Cecil made an announcement, "We are sorry to announce that the quilt raffle is postponed until the quilt can be located. We will keep you informed and thank you so much for your support and patience."

Murmurs and whispers flew through the crowd. John Colaric spoke outright and said:

"The sheriff ought to be called is what I say. It aint right that all of us who put our money in ain't got nothin'! Nothin'!"

"Oh, John, it was for a good cause, a fundraiser for the ladies, however they wanted to spend it. My guess, it will go toward War Bonds or some such thing," said Jimmie Call.

Nods went all round and the crowd thinned toward their homes and chores. It was a silent ride home for the Walkers. Their only child, Leona, was scrunched between them with Tom and Marise looking right and then left and hoping to catch sight of a yellow telltale sign of a quilt. Leona looked straight ahead and went to put her braid in her mouth, but her mom slapped her hand.

It hurt her to be sharp with this only child, but her nerves were shot. "That's enough of that, Leona! No more! I'll cut your hair off if I catch you putting it in your mouth one more time!"

"Mama, please don't…"

"Shhh! No more of that!"

Picking Up Pieces

Early 2000s, Somewhere in the Blue Ridge Mountains

"Would you look at that hillside- just covered in pink rhododendrons! It's a glorious morning full of sunshine and blue sky, and here we are the two of us back on the road again."

"Sue, we went to California and back together in 1971. What a great trip that was so long ago. Look at how the years have changed us."

"I don't know, Bonnie, that we are all that changed. Our circumstances have changed. You're a high-powered accountant with a whole region to audit, and I'm a mom of grown children, a widow after 30 years of marriage and looking at the end of the road of a teaching career."

Comfortable silence prevailed as we both thought about the life miles between us.

"Hey! Remember when Jim dared us to go in that deserted house's basement without a flashlight? He bet us ten bucks we couldn't do it."

Bonnie thought for a minute, then said:

"Gosh! What were we thinking? Good thing you brought those matches! Remember his buddies were upstairs stomping and making spooky sounds. We were supposed to find the flashlight on a workbench and then find our way back up the stairs and out. They thought we'd be screaming and wetting our pants. Ha! Fooled them, didn't we?"

"But Bonnie, our night wasn't over. We then went down the road and stole "For Sale" signs out of yards. That one man was standing in a driveway and yelled at us as we were snatching his sign. And what did we do with them? We hauled then over to Bill's house and put them all over his yard and up and down the driveway cuz he and his parents were out of town."

"Oh yeah, I remember we went in the chicken coop and took some eggs and put them on the tractor seat and covered them with straw!"

Laughter erupted. Off to the right side of the road Sue spied a weathered gray old two-story house with an overgrown yard. As they drove by, Sue said:

"Bonnie stop! Let's look at this house. We can peek in the windows. It looks deserted."

"Are you nuts?! No way!"

"Oh, c'mon, Bonnie, where's your sense of adventure? It's the middle of the day. Who's going to care if we just look around?"

Bonnie slowed down and was thinking.

"Okay, BUT we're not staying long and we're not going in that house!"

Sue laughed and clapped her hands. Bonnie pulled the car around to an almost indistinguishable driveway to the back of the house. They got out and looked around a yard full of overgrown grass and weeds with low hanging tree limbs. They saw what probably was where a barn once stood.

Sue was tall enough to look through one of the windows into a deserted old kitchen. She was right next to a stoop to a back door. She reached for the doorknob.

"Oh no you don't! I told you no way are we going in! No trouble! No- no- NO!"

"Oh geez, Bonnie! We don't even know if," (... turning the knob and door moves open) "it's open which it is! Let's just look in here. It's a back porch. Look at all the hooks on the wall for stuff to hang. The inside door is probably locked anyway. Oops! No, it isn't!"

"I'm staying right here. I'm not going in."

Sue acted like she didn't hear her and poked into the kitchen. Old wallpaper, old pink, old worn linoleum- nothing else. To the right was another empty room with old, very worn oak flooring, more old faded wallpaper. Straight ahead was the front door with a pull shade on its window. Right in front of it were the stairs to the upper floor. Sue stepped on the first stair to hear a loud crack.

Bonnie yelled, "What are you doing? Get out of there! I don't want to have to pull you out of the basement cuz you fell through!"

"Bonnie come in! There's nothing rotten here. It's in pretty good shape actually. It looks like whoever lived here just moved out and left everything clean as a whistle. Oh, just come in and see."

She started up the stairs. On the landing were doorways to either side with a door right smack at the top of the stairs. The side rooms were probably bedrooms. Light spilled in from dirty windowpanes and splashed on old linoleum floors and nothing else.

Bonnie was at the bottom of the stairs twitter pated over Sue ignoring her pleas to get out. Sue opened the door facing the stairs very cautiously only to find shelving all the way to the ceiling.

"Look, Bonnie, this was probably a storage or linen closet, don't ya think?"

"Who cares! Just get down here and get out of here!"

"All right already."

Just as she was closing the door, she looked up and thought maybe there was what looked like a little piece of yellow fabric and opened the door wide.

"Hey! I think I see something at the very top, almost touching the ceiling."

She was on her tippy toes trying to reach for it, but then decided to step on the lowest shelf like a ladder and hold on to the door frame to help her reach higher.

"SUE, what in God's name are you doing," Bonnie barked. "Bats, mice, who knows what could be up there. Stop!"

"I just want to see what's up there. Yep, I've got a hold of something. Just let me pull on it a little."

She pulled and more fabric came forward, so she pulled it out and down, making it fall to the landing.

"Sue, leave it be! Who knows what will come crawling out of it!"

What looked like an old pillowcase lay there on the floor with something stuffed in it. Sue picked it up and shook it a little and then looked in it.

"Oh, my Lord in Heaven!"

"What? What! Come down here and leave it. What are you thinking?!"

"Bonnie! There's a quilt in here! Let's take it outside and look at it. I can't believe it, can you? Who would have guessed it? I think I was supposed to come in this house. Just look what I've found!"

"Well, you can't keep it. It's not yours. You're trespassing. Put it back and let's get out of here NOW!"

"I'm not leaving it here. For what? The government probably owns the house. It's in a national park. Who's going to care about a rag?"

She closed the closet door and ran down the steps, creaking loudly. Bonnie was already out the back door and sprinting to the car when Sue carefully closed the kitchen door and then the porch door.

When she got to the car, she spilled the quilt out of its case and then shook it out. It was a quilt, in good shape too! Though heavily creased at the fold lines, it looked to have never been used. It had many squares with names embroidered in red separated by straight black embroidered lines on muslin. One name was embroidered in the center circle with names wheeling all around the circle like a starburst. The sashing was yellow as was the binding. The pencil marks were still plain as ever where the quilt had been quilted in a ripple pattern.

"Can you imagine! Just think! Wonder whose this was. It looks like a sewing club! It's dated 1941, Clarksville, West Virginia. That's just down the road a piece!"

"Shut up, Sue, and get in the car before the sheriff shows up!"

"Hang on a minute. I just want to take one last look around this place. This memory will be with me for a while."

Bonnie started the car.

Sue went over to what looked like a little mounded hill to the left of the house. She was just about to hurry back to the car with her treasure when she tripped. A bit of a rising stone poked above the weeds. Sue knelt down and looked closely. There was writing in black on the stone. In fact, it looked like a simply made tombstone. It said, Tom Walker. Pretty close to it was another with Marise Walker etched in it.

A horn honked impatiently.

Sue got up to leave, and another stone was tipped over. She turned it and pushed it back to read: Leona Walker.

Sue just looked and realized she was probably in a family cemetery and couldn't help but whisper:

"Ain't that something!"

Strike the Harp and Look in the Dumpster

The harps were sounding resonantly as Miss Young peeked through some wonderfully cottony clouds. My goodness things were busy down there on Earth! Chicago! Good Heavens! More murders every day, neighbors killing neighbors, robberies, assaults and people dying of the heat. Yes, as Peter would say, "The Devil is hard at work!"

Miss Young dared take a look over at the bank where she dedicated her life. Bank & Trust had gotten a face lift. They'd come and special washed the limestone, so it wasn't black anymore, but a special kind of grey/ white- so very nice. They put in new carpeting up to the marble flooring and columns. They had run all new electric to put in all the new machines they called computers. My goodness things had changed since she first began there as a Teller. Passbooks, paperwork, handwritten receipts done in triplicate with carbon paper! Recording transactions in a ledger each day… Press a few keys and everything is done! They didn't even need fourteen tellers anymore. Something called online made doing banking at home easier. What a world!

Bank & Trust had been good to her. She had moved by promotion to becoming Senior Loan Officer and had retired as First Vice President- quite a step for a single woman. She'd had a corner office with mahogany paneling, a private secretary, a key to a private restroom, special entrance to the executive's lunchroom, valet services, personal shopping availability, retirement pension, and stocks in the company with accumulating shares. Yes! Life at Bank & Trust had been good.

1930's/40's sweet pea quilt kit

Suddenly, a blissful feeling came over her and she had no need to look upon Earth another minute. The vibrant colors of heaven drew her attention and focus.

She looked around the lush gardens full of any number of frilly flowers. The Dahlias presently dazzled in their vibrant colors, of deep purples, brilliant yellows, soft peaches and oh, those watermelon colored dinner plate specials were too much! The friendly Cosmos congregated among the daisies and sunflowers, smiley in their faces of beauty. The many hydrangeas ballooned here and there hoping for a caress of their poofy balls of petals.

Helen doted on the sweet peas especially. Oh, the wild raspberry colored peas were lovely, but the domestic peas of pastels popping up this wall or climbing over that fence put a big grin on her face and reminded her of a special day.

She was in the Marshal Fields in the early 1940's. Pearl Harbor was tugging at her heart. So many young men at the bank had put in their notice and marched off to the recruiter's office. In the sewing, fabric and notions department she ran her fingers over some new cotton fabric thinking of starting another quilt.

Faye saw her lingering and rushed over to gush about a new shipment of quilt kits that had just been stocked.

"Oh, Helen, come over here and see the new flower line! It's a joy. What's your favorite flower? Look! Here's an applique of roses in a circle. Look, look at this Dahlia pieced in purples and lavenders. Oh, my goodness, here's a Sweet Pea kit with green leaves, stems, and vines and to-die-for pastels for the petals and buds and whole flowers."

"I've never seen kits with all the pieces precut, all the embroidery thread to match the fabric flowers. Some of these pieces are so tiny. Oh, if only I had the time."

"Time? Pshaw- what's time? Think of all the time you have- evenings and weekends! Look! This package has everything you need for two twin quilts!"

Thinking back to that afternoon, Helen was a little cross with herself for walking out of the store with a package under her arm that was going to draw her attention evermore. She was thinking about all those boys shivering on the battlefield.

She wasn't home an hour and was unpacking green binding tape also to be used for the stems and vines of the three long lines of sweet peas running vertically down the white muslin. She got her iron out and began turning back edges to pin this lovely peach petal to ready it for applique stitching. She reminded herself of her perfectionistic tendencies. Tiny, tiny hidden stitches were called for.

And so, it went. It was the late 1950's and Helen had just about completed one whole quilt top. She looked back at the last twenty years. Goodness! She had bought property and designed a three-bedroom brick ranch, which she had built. Her yard was a wonder of lush shrubs and trees with multiple beds of perennial and annual flowers. There was so much to do with work and home. She was embarrassed that she had neglected to windle down her yarn supply very much if at all. She had been flying through crocheting afghans to give the church for their bazaars and missions before her home's construction. Then the Sweet Pea project bumped into the middle of her plans. She had one quilt top pieced and completed and had started on the second one. So much to do on that one yet!

Just then, her neighbor and dearest friend, yoo-hooed across the yard.

"Hidey Ho, Helen!"

"Over here, Cathy. Just looking over these peonies. Aren't they lovely this year? When did you get home?"

"Early this morning. Seems like we've been gone forever. Look! We found this little dog on the road in Arizona. She's so sweet. We named her Cricket!"

"How does she get along in the truck?"

"Oh, she's a roadie all right."

"C'mon in and have a cup of tea, will you?"

"Well, … I guess John won't miss me for a few."

Long later Cathy had gone home, Helen sat with some crocheting in her lap. She hadn't touched it. Lately, she just sat and thought back on her life. She'd been retired for almost eight years. The bank had been firm in suggesting it was time, but what would she do? Her whole life had been wrapped up in the bank. No husband. No children. No siblings. No relatives. Oh, she had friends, best of all Cathy, and the church ladies were special, of course. She looked around the room in the evening light. There was the curio cabinet with her collection of angel figurines. Just beautiful! Her furniture was like brand new. She lemon oiled it monthly, even the piano which hadn't been opened in years. Why didn't she play anymore? Her slipper eased off her left foot and lodged on the hooked rug she'd made so many years ago. So many meaningful things tugged at her heart. What would happen to it all when it was time to step into Heaven? Oh yes, being practical and intelligent woman, she had her affairs in order.

Helen leaned over to fetch her slipper and suddenly the room went all topsy-turvy, upside down. A terrible pain pounded in her chest while her head seemed to explode and shatter.

Reverend Thomas spoke quietly in his office to Cathy and John:

"Helen was generous beyond measure. It is so good of you to see to her affairs. Once you have everything sorted, you can let me know what you will do with the house. Anything that you think will help the poor in our community, I can help you through our outreach program."

"I appreciate that. The service was lovely. She would want any and all of her yarns and fabric to go to the Women's Guild here at church. I'll be boxing it up so you can take it to the church craft/ sewing room. I'll be in touch."

Cathy was busy for weeks emptying the house. The Curio cabinet with the angels was moved into her living room. A place was found for the china and crystal in the dining room china cabinet. An estate sale was held. All else went to the church rummage sale with the exception of a box with a legal-size mail envelope that had directions, fabric pieces, and embroidery thread placed on top of the Sweet Pea quilt tops. Cathy taped the box shut and put it in her hall cedar closet, never giving it, another thought for several catastrophe filled years.

Sun poured in the Lanai and southern Florida in August powered the day. Cathy misted the Gardenias and spider plants and closed the Jalousie windows. Her intention for the day was to organize the spare bedroom and sort through boxes never opened, thus never used since moving three years ago. It was time! Gosh, it was more than time. Accumulating stuff had become a bad habit. They didn't need another thing, yet every time she went out, she came back with something. A therapist would tell her what that meant.

By the end of the day, she and her friend, Jean, had made real progress. There was a pile to go to the dumpster. Jean came out of the bedroom with a taped shut box retrieved from the closet.

"Oh, my word! I forgot all about that!"

"What's in it?"

"As I recall it is my old friend's quilt project. Let's have a look!"

Yes, there on top was the large brown envelope with various pieces of fabric to finish an applique top. They opened one quilt top to find it completed. Trailing vines with pea buds and pastel flowers expertly stitched to hidden stitch perfection made for a beautiful piece of eye work. There was a second top already started, but not nearly completed.

"Well," said Jean, "what should we do with this?"

Cathy, exhausted and decision weary, sighed and shrugged her shoulders.

"I'll have to think about it. There's nothing I can do about sewing or quilting it. Put it on the pile for now."

As it happened later on that day, there was some cloud activity and Helen took a moment to have a peek at Earth's doings. There was Cathy, sitting in the Lazy Boy with a glass of iced tea watching Home Shopping Club. Her credit card and phone were on the chair arm. Helen smiled beatifically and was about to pop back into Heaven when she froze. As she scanned the condominium environment, her eye caught a trail of sweet peas spilling out of a box precariously atop a dumpster in the parking lot.

"Now Sue, I've been told by the condominium board that there is a big problem with alligators in the complex's ponds. They've posted warnings, and I am warning you right now to be watchful and careful as you walk the paths today. Promise me?"

"No worries, Grams. I have no desire to be alligator food! I'm off. Be back in a flash and in one piece too!"

With several feet of snow in northern New York, Sue was soaking up fading sun doing a brisk power walk not missing a hat, boots, a scarf, or gloves at all. She was circling the pond by the entrance driveway keeping a wary eye for any water movement or dark shapes. She stepped up her pace and rounded on the parking lot, coming smack dab on an overflowing dumpster. She stopped to catch her breath and surveyed the rubble spilling out of the too-full container. She let out a gasp.

"Oh, my lord in heaven, it can't be!"

She reached for a sheet of colorful pastel flowers and vines falling over the rim of the dumpster.

"It's a quilt top applique!"

She stepped on the lower rim of the dumpster to reach up further. Close, but no cigar! She looked around and saw some packing boxes stacked next to the container. Pulling them over and shoving them next to the backside, her plan was to step up and look in which she did. There on top, was a legal sized envelope next to a muslin appliqued piece of fabric. She snatched that too and crawled back down.

Sue sat on the curb to investigate her find. Inside the envelope were several parcels of different colored embroidery thread, lots of cut, patterned pastel fabric pieces, and a receipt. She looked at that in wonder. It was dated 1940, Marshal Field's, "Sweet Pea Quilt Kit."

Sue said aloud:

"My lord in heaven! 2010, December, and here I've stumbled on an exquisitely finished complete quilt top and half-finished twin to it. Well, I'll be darned if that don't beat all!"

Several months later~

"Okay ladies, wait until you see what I found when I was in Florida!"

Picking Up Pieces

Betty was sitting next to her in the circle of sewing club friends, her needle raised expectantly, eyes wide open.

"Let me just get it out of this old pillowcase. I'll hold it up. Just look at this, will ya girls! Can you believe I found this in a dumpster?"

First, gasps, then an uproar of everyone talking at once exploded.

"And look! There's a twin to it, not completed though."

Eda questioned with:

"Are you going to quilt it, Sue?"

"I don't know where to begin. Got any ideas?"

Donna piped right up and said:

"Take it to an expert, right here in town. See what Rhonda thinks."

So that's what she did. She didn't launder the top or anything. She brought it to a nearby quilt shop and spread it out on the cutting table.

Some customers and sales ladies came right over and couldn't get over the expert applique work and the spectacular selection of pastels in the petal work. At 70 years old, the quilt top looked brand new:

Rhonda smoothed her hands lovingly over the trailing flowers. She put her glasses on and looked closely at the stitching.

"Oh my! I've never seen anything like this. It's heavenly!"

She was quiet and just looked all over the piece before finally saying:

"I'd love to custom machine quilt this in an echo- like style. Would you consider letting me do it? It would be such an honor to work on this that I will give you a special price. Please, let me do it."

Sue knew that custom quilting charged by the square inch. It didn't matter to her. It would be worth it to have an expert do it who so obviously valued the quilt.

"Okay! It's yours for the doing. No rush. No deadline. Take your time. Call me when you need me to pick it up."

It wasn't too long before the call came for pick up.

I entered the shop to find clerks and patrons gathered around the Sweet Pea Quilt. There were so many approving comments, again remarking on the superior stitching of the applique. I locked onto their faces and couldn't help but wonder if the sewer herself wasn't happy to look down from heaven and see the beauty of her completed creation and smile in satisfaction.

Susan Frazier

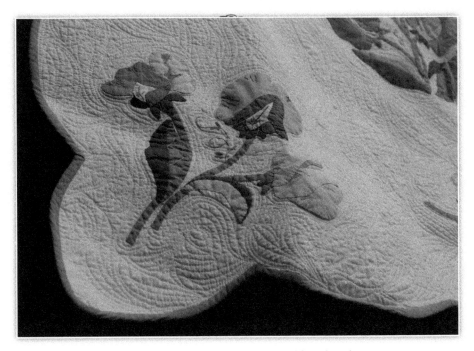

sweet pea quilt corner-custom quilted by Rhonda Loy

Lord, Help Me

Morning sun peeked over the tree line as Rosemary pulled the water hose toward the garden. She turned the brass nozzle to a fine showering mist and pointed it to the daisies, lilies, and milkweeds. Mommy wanted those milkweeds pulled out, but Rosie whined that the monarch butterflies loved them and used them to lay their eggs. So, they stayed. The water mist created an iridescent cast across the ground. Suddenly, a hummingbird flashed through the water. It was ruby throated and flitted in and out of the water seemingly to first drink and then get wet. It flew to the hydrangea bush where it began to preen and clean itself oblivious to Rosie's presence. At one point it hummed right up to her shoulder mistaking her red blouse for something good to drink. She thought back to another day on the ranch long ago long before there were hoses with brass nozzles…

"There's some bagged cotton bolls in the grain room that need to be carded and readied for a batting for a quilt or two. You need to move them to the house."

"Ah geez! Can't it wait? Let me get things watered before it gets so hot."

"No! Daddy's bringing in some grain sacks and wants this cleared out."

"Oh, okay. Bye-bye Mr. Ruby Throat."

The barn smelled sweetly of new mown hay. The wagons had brought it in piled high and then pitched it in the mow. Daddy said he saw a new machine at the expo that gathered up the cut hay, packed it somehow, put string around it and spit out a square bale.

Mommy could tell right away that he was figuring on how much it would cost and whether he could get his hands on one. She pursed her lips and kept still. It was useless to talk economy once Daddy got a notion about wanting something.

It was that way with the thresher and the milk separator and that John Deere tractor that worked the plow so dandily. She wished the Farm Journal would blow across the field each month, even if it did have some really good recipes and advice from farm women. He wouldn't get to see all those advertisements about this new gadget or that thingamabob that he would set to wanting. There were only so many families in town that bought her eggs or fancied her floral vases full of Zinnias and Black Eyed Susans. The sweet cream, when it could be, had brought in a few cents more, thankfully. Her needlework was in demand too. The flour and sugar sacks were a welcome boon for the shirts, blouses, bloomers, curtains, and such she worked on in the evening. Now that the feed sacks were coming in colors and patterns, not just white anymore, she had a whole new opportunity to make dresses, aprons, and work shirts. It was kind of fun too. Her work was in demand, and she was proud to be able to contribute to the farm and family.

There was something else Peggy was proud of too. Quilting! Her momma and aunts had all been quilters and she'd learned from the best. She'd started with just little patches to patch a doll quilt. How many times had Aunt Mamie made her rip the crooked, irregular stitches out? Pretty soon though, she was making baby pieced quilts and not nearly so much having to rip threads.

There was a neighbor woman who sometimes stopped by while walking to town. The whole family loved her stories. One time she told them, back in the day when she and Issac first laid eyes on this Texas ground and dug themselves a little Soddy as their first home. She figured she spent three months out here all alone with the chickens and cow they brought with them while her man was hauling freight from the train station up to the hills where the mines were. Margaret didn't know a soul. Nobody lived within ten miles of their spread. Once she got the garden planted, she decided to dig a little more under the Soddy. She humped the prairie grass up on top of the pine logs on the floor. The chickens were scratchin' for bugs and worms and cackling at her.

"Go on- Git!"

One hen just moved behind her as if supervising the excavation.

If anybody'd asked, Margaret would have explained how underneath the house (Soddy) would be a good place in the winter for animals. No barn yet! No coop! Just slabs of dirt piled on top of each other. Grass roots were holding it all together. God only knew what it would be like next spring, but there would be cover for humans and animals alike. Maybe the heat from the beasts would rise up into the house. She had stitched together big patches of fabric ripped from Isaac's worn out work pants and coats. She didn't put any filler in these blankets, just a backing and then knotted it with brown packing string. She could use these for tarps or ground covers at picnics. She had a mind to use them on the floor come winter. She was thinking some of the really old, frayed, tattered quilts could be hung on the walls. The tar paper on the outside didn't do much to keep the cold out.

These blanket makings took up her time more than any piecing of what she thought of as pretty quilts. Besides, she didn't have many pieces in her stash bag. No friends or relatives were around to give her any of these scraps either. She would just make do.

Make do? How? The only things in her stash bag were a paper with needles, some brown cord- like thread, and Isaac's one-shot pistol, small as can be. She kept it in the bag and the bag on her lap most usually.

That day she had made corn bread in the Dutch oven on the little fire in the yard by the stoop. It would be all she could hope to eat with the eggs for the next couple days. She sat on the ground with her back against the stoop which was no more than some flat rocks stacked up. The sun was bright but not overly hot and it was hard not to take a little snooze. She started humming the tune to "Clementine" and pretty soon broke into the words finishing with, "Dreadful sorry, Clementine." She thought for a minute and smiled. She was just fixin' to start in on "How Great Thou Art" when…

Margaret looked out across the plains and saw a dust kick up aways apiece. She squinted and her heart leaped hoping it might just be Isaac. She shaded her eyes and pulled her prairie bonnet down to see better. It wasn't his horse; in fact, it looked to be a mule. Nobody from around here had a mule. Tweren't long before the man rode up in the yard. He didn't dismount, but looked down at her and said:

"Howdy! Where's your man?"

Before she could answer, he then said:

"Corn bread! I'd shore like me some of that! Get it for me and a big drink of water!"

Margaret had a little shiver go through her. This man was filthy, grubby, nearly toothless, rags for clothes, stinking to the high heavens and ordering her around.

She didn't move.

"Did ya hear me? Are ya deaf or just dumb?"

She didn't respond.

"I guess I'll just get down and show ya what I mean ya to do!"

At that she said:

"Whoa there fella! My man will be here anytime now. He won't take kindly to you acting so meanly."

"Lady! There ain't no man here nor comin'! Look! Miles of flat land all around and ain't one speck or cloud anywhere to be seen. Who are you kiddin'? Hitch yourself up and do as I say. I got some plans for you, I shore do!"

With that he slipped down and grinning with a leer lurched toward her.

Margaret instinctively put her had in her stash bag which he noticed and said:

"Watcha got in your little poke bag? Maybe some money? You'd better just throw it right here!"

And he made to grab it or her.

Ka Boom!

Margaret closed her eyes and heard the oomph next to her and felt dirt spray in her face. When she opened her eyes, she stared at a hole between two rheumy eyes and a cavernous rotten open mouth with spittle drooling down the corner of cracked brown lips.

"Lord help me!"

Margaret sat there dazed for a while, but the mule was pawing at the ground and acted thirsty. She hoisted herself up and stepped over the weasel of a lump and grabbed the reins to lead the thirsty animal over the wooden water trough.

Standing there, she noticed a rotted-out burlap bag rolled up behind the saddle. Margaret shook its contents out on the ground. A knotted sock cashinckled in a coin-like noise. A graniteware cup and plate with crusted decayed grime on it fell out. A shirt that was filthy with no buttons tumbled out. Nothing else! No evidence of a name- nothing.

The chickens scratched at the shirt looking for fleas or ticks maybe.

Margaret thought for a while and decided to get her a rope. She put the chickens in the pen and put the rope on Hildy and walked her over to the lump with flies congregating on the face. She figured on going to the neighbors. If Hildy was docile enough, maybe she could fling the body on her back like a sack and get on the mule.

She went in the soddy, tidied it up, put what she considered precious in a pillowcase, and picked up the hole eaten sock without even looking at its contents. Her stash bag had a hole in it and the gun was still in it with some needles, brown cord and some worn fabric pieces.

She pulled Hildy and tied the lead to the post. She put her hands on her hips and with her toe of her boot kicked the lump over, so his face was kissing the ground. Rigor mortis hadn't set in, so she grabbed him under his arms and marveled at how small and light he was. She flung him over Hildy's back. Her tail twitched furiously, but she didn't buck, kick or shy away. Margaret scratched her ears and thanked her for being so helpful.

Peggy's and John's place was ten miles down the road to the east. She wasn't walking this time so she didn't know how long it would take.

The sun was setting when Peggy looked up and saw a figure on a horse with a cow trailing it with something on its back. She called:

"John! Someone's coming up the lane."

Rosemary and Bill came to the porch to see. Rosemary looked hard.

"Mommy, I think it's Margaret!"

John said:

"What in tarnation!" and ran toward her.

Margaret pulled up with a huge sigh of relief. She needed help getting down from the saddle and nearly fell at first.

Bill's eyes were big as saucers as he spied the lump on Hildy who by now was not having anything more to do with it and summarily half bucked it off with a satisfying smack to the ground.

Peggy already had a glass of water and was helping Margaret to the house while John had his hat off scratching his head.

Bill and Rosemary took Hildy to the barn, gave her some hay and water, and milked her. Bill said:

"Who do you suppose that is, Rosie?"

"Beats me! Did you ever see such a mess of a man?"

"Peggy, now that I'm here, I wonder if I should've come at all. Lord in heaven! Look at what I've done! I'm thinking I could've just dug a hole and thrown the louse in and nobody would be the wiser."

"Margaret, dear, are you hungry? Would you like a wet towel for your face and neck? Don't talk yet. Just settle down. We can hear all about it later."

Later came after a couple hours, Margaret was refreshed, and the body had been dragged behind the cottonwoods to the west.

"Now what?"

John replied:

"Well, we don't know who he is or where he came from. You did what you needed to do to protect yourself. I say we put him in the ground and call it a day. When Isaac comes, we can tell him, I guess. We'd like you to stay here with us for a while. We can take our wagon back to your soddy, get your chickens, and pick up whatever you need to have with you. How does that sound?"

Margaret nodded weakly and was glad to have someone else make decisions. She was plum wore out.

Weeks went by and still no word or sign of Isaac. Peggy had fixed up a little room off the kitchen for Margaret and life settled around the five of them. A letter from Caddo County Mining Company came with a terse message that Isaac had been in an accident with a loaded wagon and after two days had "bit the dust."

John sat on the porch one evening, rocking just a little while Peggy mended a shirt of his. She was going to secure the buttons better too. John was slow to speak, but he'd been figuring in his head for a while. As he was fixing to share his new idea with Peggy, Margaret came out of the house wiping her hands on her apron. He stopped rocking and leaned forward and said, "Margaret, I was just about to talk to Peggy about an idea I got. Since it concerns you, a part of it anyway, I'd like you to sit and listen."

"Course I will! With ready ears!"

John pulled his socks up and wiggled his toes, nudged his boots aside, and cleared his throat.

"Ya see, I've got an idea about this here land, it's got water! A lot of it! The best natural water for miles around. It's been good to us and for us. I was thinking if we added some land, we could get some cattle and section off to rotate grazing needs. We'd have to put up posts and string wire, lots of it, but it would make for a heck of a cattle ranch.

I read whereas this country grows beef is going to be in demand. We might just as well get in on the supply train."

Peggy interrupted and said," Now John, you're talking a lot of money, time, and work. We're going to need more land, more help, more money, more..."

John put his hand on her arm, patting it and shushing her.

"I know, I know. We got a little money saved. I thought we could take on a partner."

"A partner?! Who?"

John slowly turned his head toward Margaret and said:

"That's why I wanted you sitting here. You know how well we all get along. Ever since you came, you're one of the family and…"

Margaret put her hand up to stop his speaking.

"You couldn't be more like family if you were blood to me. Where would I be? I, too, been thinking. You know Isaac and I figured on building our homestead into something worth keeping and even having some kids to be a part of it all. Government says we have to work it to keep it. How am I gonna do that? So, yes, coming to a partnership with you and Peggy would please me fine. I got the back pay and settlement from Isaac's mining company, AND who'd a thought that sock money would be so much. I say we got a stake in a cattle ranch together!'

Peggy smiled to herself and wondered if her egg money would continue to be needed, but she hugged Margaret like she would her mother or best friend already thinking about fixing up the bunkhouse. Between hers and Margaret's quilts, there would be bedding and hanging insulation.

***Quilts found on bunk house and ranch house walls
from civil war into new century.***

It was 1999 when Chris and Debbie pulled into my driveway. They got out of the car with some cloth bundles. They had been out to the ranch in South-West Oklahoma and brought some things from the ranch house and bunkhouse swaddled up in some musty smelling, bedraggled, very worn quilts.

Picking Up Pieces

Chris told me there was some crockery wrapped up in the quilts and that I should throw the rags on the burn pile when I get them unwrapped.

Well, I didn't!! I put them folded up on a shelf in the garage until my husband told me to decide what's to be done with them. They smelled horribly. So, I washed them! What harm could be done? They were destined for the burn pile.

I air dried the three quilts by hanging them over the porch railing. One was particularly threadbare; Chris said that it had been hung on the wall of the bunkhouse, probably for insulation. All were quilted with thick brown cord-like thread. I'm sure they were lovely one time, long ago. Even with the brown thread, one was geometrically intricate. Another had brown checked or red plaid pieces still in good shape.

I had the opportunity to go to an appraisal event nearby. A textile expert was present. She told me, in her opinion, the quilts were from the latter half of the nineteenth century and the brown checked one was probably Civil War vintage.

These three quilts came from great, great grandparents' homestead where cattle roamed and rattlesnakes slithered. Where John and Peggy, Rosemary, Bill, and a woman named Margaret, looking for Isaac roamed, played, laughed, and cried.

authenticated civil war fabric

Susan Frazier

Aren't We Something!

Carol asked me if when I came over would I drive my truck. The community garage sale was over, and what was left wasn't coming back in the house. So, could I take it with my stuff to Goodwill?

Really wasn't much but a few boxes, and I planned to go through the house one more time to look for "uncluttering items."

Once home, I pushed some of the boxes closer together and in doing so tipped one over. What jumbled out got my interest. A white pair of petticoats, hand-made with hooks and eyes, lace, non-elastic waistband, and one really wasn't a petticoat but a crotchless pair of drawers- "underpants." There was a pair of black stockings with the manufacturer's tag still on the upper hem, never worn! But what really caught me was a kaleidoscope of velvety colors and wonderful fancy embroidery. I pulled out what was a crazy quilt in perfect condition. What was this doing in the "give it to charity" box? Wait! There was more. I knelt, pulled out another thin, much used patchwork crazy quilt made from cotton fabrics of old shirts, blouses, dresses, old remnant cloth, etc. It had a faded patterned backing, but it had decorative embroidery just as the more than very nice velvet crazy quilt. Other than they were both crazy quilts, there was no comparison.

Welp, this box isn't going anywhere! I was going to do some investigating.

Bertha sat on her bed and gripped the bedpost tightly. Voices were murmuring below as mother's friends gathered for tea. She would have to go down soon or risk her mother's tongue lashing. Why couldn't she just stay up here and look at her handkerchief collection? She could lay them all out on the bed and sort them again. By far she had many white hankies with all kinds of edging crocheted, tatting, lace, hand rolled, and stitched. There were embroidered flowers, and white on white designs. She just loved them all.

"Bertha!"

She looked up startled to see her mother at her door and slowly rose to follow her wordlessly down to the lions.

Flora Ethridge was sitting on the settee and cackled to her to come over and sit right next to her.

"Oh Lord," thought Bertha, "give me strength."

"Now girl, what are you eating? You are nothing but bones! Goodness! Load up on some of my cake! It'll do you good. Look at your hair! It's fine and wispy. You need to pad and pat it up with some of your hair pulled from your brush. Men like a woman with a head of hair all curled and loaded up. Maybe you should wash it with eggs, give it some shine. You don't have any bosoms either! Land sakes, you know you could stuff some pulled cotton in your corset to plump up what's not much."

Bertha got up with apologies that she needed to help her mother.

She escaped to the kitchen and found her younger cousin, Elsie, arranging scones she'd brought from the farm along with fresh butter and even fresh cream.

"Hi, Bert!" Elsie was the only one who addressed her with a pet name. It wasn't allowed by her parents- "undignified!"

"Oh, Elsie, thank God you're here. These teas are unbearable! Why do these women feel inclined to swoop down on me and offer advice as to how to get a man?!"

"Well, Bert, let's get them fed and up to the Bridge table. Then we can make our escape! Okay?"

Bertha nodded and began piling molasses cookies on a plate. She checked the spooner to see that there were more than enough spoons. She took the tray with carefully folded tea napkins and carried it to the buffet.

Women were already choosing which table of players they would like to pair with. Cut glass water pitchers were on the buffet with matching glasses. Fancy teacups with saucers were at the tables already. Boiling water was on the stone waiting to be poured into warmed tea pots.

Later, as the girls were giggling over Mrs. Higgenbottom's ridiculous hat that had what looked like toadstools piled on it, Bert confided in Elsie how terribly uncomfortable these women made her feel. Her mother never came to her defense either. Dorothy Huber had whispered to her today, that ugly ducklings didn't stay ugly ducklings.

Elsie leaned toward Bert and said, "Bert, what is so fascinating about your handkerchiefs? You have so many. Why?"

Bert gripped the seams of her dress and smoothed them while she thought for a minute and then said:

"Well, my grandma had a whole drawer full. She took a fresh one every day and tucked it in her belt at her waist or in her sleeve. She had everyday ones, going out during the day hankies, church hankies, and party or dress up ones. She had lots of plain white hankies, lots with embroidery, some with crocheted edges, others with lace and tatting, and many just too beautiful to use except to be seen. She let me help her fold them after they were washed and ironed. Then she would put them neatly in the drawer. Once she had me count them. 78 hankies!

She told me that handkerchiefs were used a long time ago to convey secrets to friends and beaus. That holding them a certain way or placing them in such a way in your hand or near your face could send a message.

Hankies were used in books to create tension in a plot. For instance, if one were dropped strategically, an appointment to return it to the lady who dropped it would have to be made, thus, allowing for a contrived meeting.

It was a hankie in Shakespeare's *Othello* that moved Iago's most evil plot to intensify the jealousy that eventually killed Desdemona. Now that my grandma's gone, I just like to remember her with hankies. I feel like a part of her is still with me. If I try real hard, I can sometimes smell the liniment she rubbed on her knees, not that it smelled all that good!"

The girls laughed and were startled by the appearance of a gentleman before them.

"Pardon me, ladies. I am sorry to surprise you, but I am here to take my mother home. I may be just a little early. I am Edwin Peterson. Edna Peterson is my mother. And may I ask whom I have the pleasure of coming upon under this magnificent chestnut tree?"

"Bertha turned red and tucked her chin into her neck and worried the wadded-up hanky in her hand. It was Elsie who giggled and introduced them to Edwin. She offered the plate of cookies from the blanket on the ground to him. When he selected one, a call from the house signaled to the girls to come in and say their goodbyes to the leaving ladies.

"Well, Miss Bertha and Miss Elsie- until we meet again, goodbye," smiled Edwin.

It was weeks later when Bertha's mom came onto the porch where Bertha was reading and announced that Mrs. Peterson and her son, Edwin, had invited the three of them to dinner on Wednesday evening. To which Bertha attempted to extricate herself from the invitation by saying she really didn't see why she should be included.

Her mother replied, "Bertha, it is time you worked at attempting to be social. Heavens you only go to church and to Mrs. Fisher's Lending Library. You never do anything with the girls from town. It's time you took part in some things where you meet others and have conversations."

"Oh, Mother! What do I have to talk about? My canary? She sings so beautifully every morning at breakfast. I don't care a fig about the clothes you have Mrs. Roskilley fashion for me, and neither would anyone else, except maybe Elsie. So, wherever I go, I wind up being a wallflower."

Wednesday evening found Mrs. Peterson seated at the head of the table with Edwin on her right and Bertha to his right. Bertha's father was to Edna's left with his wife to his left.

Bertha fidgeted with her napkin in her lap while dinner table talk droned on about the weather then switched to the plans to build a gazebo in the town square park, all while sipping cool cucumber soup. Bertha was releasing a sigh of relief as she excused herself from the table for a breath of fresh air. She moved through the spacious front doors of the grand Victorian home to the gingerbread front porch. She leaned against the railing and took a deep breath. Whew! Why did dinner have to take so long, she wondered.

She unwadded the hanky in her fist and shook it out over the flowerbed. The horrid peas fell to the ground unceremoniously. Good! The mice and chipmunks could gag on them. She would wash and rinse grandma's tattered hanky when she got home.

"Miss Bertha?" Bertha looked up to find Edwin at her elbow.

"Yes?"

"I was going to walk around the yard and wondered if you would accompany me."

Bertha tucked her chin into her neck and was protesting before he finished that she was feeling lightheaded and would be unsuitable company. Edwin acted as if he hadn't heard her and was taking her elbow and smiling at her.

He moved her down the stairs and toward the side yard. He was actually humming a waltz tune quietly. He stepped to touch some of the flowers along the walkway.

Bertha noticed that Edwin didn't release her elbow. She commented on the zinnias and the variety of colors shaded against the boxwoods.

"You know your flowers, Miss Bertha, you surely do. Where did you come to learn about them?"

Bertha hesitated a second and decided she could talk without worrying about being criticized or dismissed by an adult.

"My grandma was a natural in the garden. She had a rose garden that all of her friends envied. Her bouquets were on the church altar every Sunday. Her zinnias, cleomes, and snapdragons were colorful and plentiful. She was a wonder and taught me a lot."

About that time, they had come to the chicken yard and Edwin said, "My dad just loved these chickens. He raised them from chicks hatched every spring. Look here! This is a Rhode Island Red. Isn't she pretty? Look at her feathers and how she puffs them. Look at her eyes. They're clear and bright. She doesn't miss a thing, sort of like you, Miss Bertha."

He was smiling at her when he said this and then all of a sudden, he picked the hen up and was holding and petting it. She liked it and was clucking, not squawking.

Bertha hesitantly reached to pet her. The bird let her, which made Bertha giggle with delight and Edwin responded by saying, "Why, you two are friends! My dad named his chickens. I'm going to name this one after you- Miss Bertha." Bertha's face turned red, but she was pleased and tucked her chin into her neck and grinned sheepishly. She could barely wait to see Elsie and tell her.

"Bertha! Bertha! Berr-thaa!" Her dad was calling her.

Picking Up Pieces

example of lace edged handkerchiefs of the age

"Edwin went to the walkway and said, "She's here, sir.""

"We will be going home now. Come along, girl."

Edwin put Miss Bertha down, and retrieved Bertha's elbow to her secret dismay. When he helped her into the carriage, he smiled and said, "Miss Bertha, I've been most delighted with being in your company this evening. Thank you."

Bertha mis stepped and nearly tumbled into the carriage wheel, dropping her handkerchief to the ground, unseen by anyone. Embarrassed by her clumsiness, Bertha mumbled an apology and hurriedly took her seat.

Her father said, "Giddy up, Millie. Thank you and your mother, Edwin."

That evening went a long way to put a blush on Bertha's cheeks. Edwin had actually said he enjoyed her company. Really?! If only she hadn't dropped grandma's handkerchief. It was one of her favorites.

On Wednesday morning the postman delivered an envelope addressed to Bertha who had never received any mail ever. It must be an address mistake. She opened the envelope to read a card that said, "Mrs. Peterson and her son, Edwin, wish to visit at 2 o'clock on Friday. A favor of a reply would be appreciated."

Bertha's mother waited expectantly to know the contents of the missive. She tried to hide her surprise upon hearing the request to visit.

"Goodness! I wonder what this is about. I'll have to have some tea and lemonade, and perhaps, cookies too. We can receive them on the veranda, I think."

"Oh, Mother, this is nothing but a polite way to spend an otherwise nothing-to-do afternoon."

Bertha secretly was curious and a little atwitter. No one ever asked to visit her, least of all a man. Of course, his mother had written the note.

"I'll send a reply and sign both of our names. Bertha you must wear that new floral dress Miss Louise just delivered. We'll wash your hair in the morning. Oh, isn't this so lovely! We are having visitors!"

Elsie came Friday morning to help in the kitchen and planned to be available to serve in the afternoon. She and Bertha were upstairs, and the preparations going on would have made anyone think the Queen of England was coming. Bertha's mom was making a big deal.

Bertha was pleased with her new dress. It was of the softest pale yellow with the tiniest of violets sprinkled all over, and little rows of lace trickled down from her neck to her waist. It caused her eyes to have a steely gray shade to them that Elsie talked her into highlighting with a little kohl.

Bertha reddened when Elsie snatched some hankies from her drawer and carefully tucked them in her upper corset.

"Oh Bertie! No worries. Everyone does it! Let me brush your hair for you. How about if instead of a bun, I roll your hair into a French Twist with tendrils by your ears? Wear your grandma's pearl ear buttons, won't you?!" As Bertha descended the stairs, she looked in the mirror at a stranger. Her cheeks colored and she found herself tucking her chin into her neck. Why did she do that? She told herself to stop it immediately. It made her look stupid. When her mother saw her, she couldn't hide her pleasure.

"Why Bertha! Look how pretty you look. We should have visitors every day! Maybe now you'll take an interest in getting some new clothes."

With a lovely white handkerchief with embroidered violets at the corners nestled in her lap, Bertha sat in a wicker chair on the veranda and watched the Peterson's carriage pull up to the front walk. Edwin tied the horse to the hitching post with the iron ring and helped his mother down ever so carefully. Elsie met them at the door and showed them to the veranda after they dropped their calling cards in the glass basket in the foyer.

Bertha and her mom greeted them politely and offered them seats on the white wicker chairs with floral cushions.

Bertha tried very hard not to stare at Edwin who seemed to be trying very hard not to stare at her. He wore a very nice fitting charcoal gray suit with a tiny pin striped baby blue shirt. His collar was starched, and the collar buttons were gold. He had a very slim build and very fine boned hands which he kept in his lap.

Pleasantries were exchanged; the weather was remarked on with a hope for rain soon. It was then that Edwin established the reason for the visit.

"Miss Bertha, the other night while you were over at our house, you dropped your handkerchief and I wished to make its safe return to you today. He pulled a tissue packet from his pocket and handed it to her. She opened it to find her grandma's hanky, freshly laundered, starched and ironed. Her face shone with delight at seeing it again.

"Oh my! Thank you ever so much, Edwin. I wondered where it went, and I am ever so happy to have it back as it was my grandmother's," she beamed gratitude.

At that moment Edwin stood up and said, "Ladies, if I may be so bold as to ask if you would join me in a carriage ride around town and in the park by the lake. It's a lovely day for a drive, don't you think?"

The ladies twittered at the notion but gathered their gloves and made for the carriage. Bertha without a thought stood to get in the front seat while the moms sat in the back together. It was lovely on a lovely day to drive through the town at a trot creating a slight breeze and be seen by many curious townspeople.

Mrs. Collins came out of the bank and was startled to see Mr. Peterson, the owner of the drug store, driving three ladies through town in the middle of the afternoon. Who was that girl in the seat beside him laughing so? Mrs. Decker sidled up to her and remarked, "Sylvia Collins, do you see Mrs. Peterson and her son with Mrs. Finlan and her daughter in that carriage? It's the middle of the afternoon on a Friday for heaven's sake! Where can they be going?"

Edwin took a turn to the park and slowed the horse to a walk. He could see Bertha was enjoying herself and the ladies were pleased as punch to be taking in the air.

Bertha saw Tillie and Jewell stand and gape at her as they passed. Wasn't this something? She, Bertha Finlan, sitting in a carriage next to Mr. Edwin Peterson. Imagine that!

Bertie and Elsie were leaning up against the gate at the Peterson's chicken coop while their moms were gathered for another afternoon social. Bertie had shared her story of Edwin countless times with Elsie and now had the chance to introduce her namesake to her.

"Look Elsie! She's coming right over to me like she remembers me. Edwin says she has sharp, clear eyes like mine. You know what he said to me when we were driving around town? He said he thought I was very observant, and he liked how I listened and looked thoughtful. And you know what else, Elsie? Edwin said he liked my hair and the way it curled by my ears."

Elsie hugged Bertie and smiled at her. She noticed how Bertie had smiled at her. She noticed how Bertie stood straighter and smiled more and didn't tuck her chin into her neck anymore.

"Elsie, you know what I did last week? I went to the library and looked at some books on raising chickens. There's a ton of details on doing it. Edwin learned everything from his dad who loved his chickens. Though, he called it a hobby. Elsie, I read about the best way to set up a coop. You have to have ventilation and regulate air drafts and keep the nests up off the ground and have boards for them to roost. You've got to keep them safe from varmints, and my gosh, Elsie, feeding them is a science! If you take good care of them, depending on what breed they are, you can get 265 eggs a year from one chicken!"

"My goodness, Bertie, you are so excited. Your cheeks are rosy. You know what else, Bertie? You haven't talked about handkerchiefs once today. Oh! And you know what else? Mrs. Roskilly told my mother that you came into her shop and had three new dresses made. You never cared a fig for what you were wearing!"

Just as Bertie started to respond, she looked up to see Edwin pulling up to the barn.

He tied his horse to the post and walked right over to the girls with a big smile.

"Why ladies, whatever are you doing out here with my chickens?" he asked.

"Bertie was introducing me to Miss Bertha."

"Bertie?" said Edwin quizzically.

Bertha turned to him and laughingly said, "Oh Elsie calls me that- has forever."

"Well now, since we are discussing names. Why don't you ladies pick a chicken and give it a name. Go ahead Elsie. Which one catches your eye? Maybe that one by Miss Bertha?" Edwin offered.

Elsie giggled at the thought of naming a chicken but saw a black and white checkered hen come up to the fence and almost yelled, "Miss Agnes! That's Miss Agnes! Oh, can she be Miss Agnes? She reminds me of my grandma's sister."

"Miss Agnes it is," laughed Edwin and then he turned and said, "Bertie, what about you? Which one has caught your eye?"

Bertie? Bertie? Elsie was the only one who had ever called her that.

Bertie looked at Edwin and was glad to see him looking kindly at her and encouraging her to say something.

"Oh, let me see. Look at that cinnamon colored one over there. The whole time we've been here, she's been scratching and pecking. She hasn't paid one bit of attention to us until you came up, Edwin. She's just busy. I'll call her Mamie! My grandmother's name was Mae, but my grandfather fondly called her 'Mamie'."

Just then Mamie looked at her and stopped scratching and just clucked to which they all laughed.

Bertie, then rather quietly said to Edwin, "Edwin, what do you do to prevent your flock from being wiped out by coccidiosis?"

Edwin was startled and looked at her in dismay. How in the world would she know?

"Why, Bertie, coccidiosis is a parasite that occurs with poor nutritional intake and an unclean yard and coop. So, my dad was a stickler about buying good feed with additives from the mill and keeping our yard and coop very sanitary. Elsie's dad happily cleans and removes the chicken waste to use in their garden. He brings in sand to the yard so mud and waste can't build up."

Bertie looked wistfully at the birds and said, "I'd just hate for these girls to get sick, Edwin. You would miss them, too. They remind you of your father, I am sure of it. Her voice trembled a little, thinking of her grandma and how much she missed her. Edwin noticed her eyes welling up and put his hand on her shoulder while reaching in his pocket and offering her his handkerchief. She held it and as she wiped her eyes, she caught the scent of cinnamon, maybe? She attempted to return it and reached in her pocket for her own hanky, but Edwin folded her hand around it and patted her back gently while saying, "Keep it, Bertie."

Bertie sat at the kitchen table contemplating those oh so long-ago memories. In her hands was a man's hanky, monogrammed with an 'E'. Edwin had wiped her eyes at the chicken yard with it. He used many handkerchiefs thereafter. Before the fashion of gloves came on the scene, he would use a handkerchief between his hand and Bertie's ball gown so as to not leave a perspiration stain on the fabric. Elsie's mom had told her that a woman never returned a handkerchief to a man, but a man always saw it returned to a woman.

Just then Elsie rapped at the door and popped in with a big laundry basket. "Elsie, what have you got there?"

"Oh Bertie, just look. I got it all finished! Thanks ever so much for letting me borrow Miz Peterson's parlor crazy quilt. It's such a fine crazy quilt with all those rich velvets. Mine don't have any such in it. Look, here. It's Missy's little dress and here's my old blouse remnants. Look I had left over goods to make the backing from the bedroom curtains I made a while ago. I practiced and copied the embroidery stitches like Miz P's."

"Elsie!" Bertie giggled. "Mrs. Peterson would frown at you calling her Miz P."

"Oh posh, Bertie! Edwin went a far piece loosening up this here house, especially after his mother passed and you became the only Mrs. Peterson. Anyway, let me get your quilt back to its place in the parlor on the settee where everybody always saw it and admired it. Mine will be used on Missy's bed. She likes it right fine."

"Oh Elsie, I'm just happy that you enjoyed making it and will make it useful. Mother Peterson never once used hers but only to look at. It's just as it was the day Mrs. Roskilly brought it in that tissue paper box. Edwin said it became her prized possession. It'll be yours and Missy's if anything ever happened to Edwin and me. We don't have any children to pass our things to. Relatives will have to sort this house out."

"Barb! Here's a box. It's got two old quilts, a mink muff, some really old petticoats, and a pair of never worn black cotton stockings with the tags still on. Where should I put it? Oh! There's a box of vintage handkerchiefs, too!"

"Give it to Carol. She can put it in her basement. Maybe her kids will want to play with them."

poor woman's copy of the crazy quilt

Picking Up Pieces

Bits and Pieces

Susan Frazier

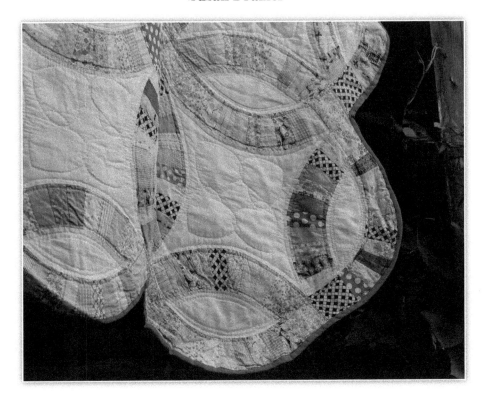

Double Wedding Ring Quilt

This was a top that I found in a box under a table in an Indiana antique shop. I was with my mother in law and on a whim got off the highway and stopped. I picked it up and put it back down several times having been drawn to it. The shop owner came over and commented that he noticed I had taken a liking to it. Ann said I should get it and finish it, but I put it back.

He said, "Look, I've had that here a long time and nobody has favored it as you have today. It's yours for $10."

I quilted it in the same way my great grandmother had done my parent's wedding quilt and all the while I felt a presence as I stitched. That's when I first got the feeling that I was making a woman very happy, by finishing her quilt made up of old blouses, shirts, skirts, curtains, and dresses.

Trip Around the World Quilt

Done in greens and golds, this quilt came to me completely finished and in great shape as a king-sized quilt. My friend, Millie Howlett, bought a raffle ticket on the quilt for one dollar. It was made by the Howell St. Joseph's Women's Quilting Guild and offered as a Melonfest fundraiser. Millie won it- the only thing she ever won. Millie is in love with all things Victorian, including rose and burgundy and beige colors. She did not have a king-sized bed. She kept the quilt through several moves without really using it until finally deciding to give it to me, noting my quilt affection. It would have a safe home with me.

Floral Red and Black Interest Quilt

I was asked to create an instructional display of quilt making and quilt history information for a flower show exhibition. The show had a quilt theme throughout. Upon arrival at the hall, a woman, Linda, attached herself to me quite quickly. She showed me the many quilts she had on display which were varied and quite beautiful. I was struck by how she treated me as an old friend immediately. I had brought quite a few quilting themed books to give away throughout the three-day show. Linda took them all! The last day of the show arrived as did I, to collect my display of several quilts for "Show and Tell" display. On the wall by my display hung a brilliant red with black highlights floral quilt made by none other than Linda!

She was still quite attached to me which I paid attention to and wondered why I found myself in her space. I commented on her quilt and admired it verbally. I watched her face and without thinking blurted out an offer to buy the quilt from her. (I had no intention of buying a quilt!) Linda's face became so animated it glowed. She was delighted to hear I liked it enough to buy it. We agreed on a price while I continued to marvel at my unexplained, unplanned purchase. It was as if some force had brought us together in a spiritual plan.

And then she sighed heavily as she patted her quilt and said, "I can pay my taxes tomorrow."

Crazy Quilt Wall Hanging

I had admired a quilt wall hanging quilt at the home of a friend several years ago. The quilt was also a part of an exhibition at a flower show at one time. Recently Mary offered to give me the quilt.

I questioned her about its origin. Her early family was prominent in Indiana. Her grandfather had been a banker. His suit linings and pocket liners and ties became pieces for the six panels to which were added brocades, silks, and velvets and then embroidered heavily in the crazy quilt stitches of feather stitch, chicken foot, or spider web, traditional to the late 1800s .

Hard times forced the family to move to Central Lake, Michigan where Mr. Malone came to be in charge of the canning factory. In the early 70s, Mary's mother commissioned a woman to sew the panels into a framed by strips of brown velvet whole piece to which loops were sown so that the quilt could be hung as a piece of art.

As Mary began eliminating and downsizing her home, she was stymied by what to do with this family treasure. A sister, a brother, a son, a daughter? None wanted the quilt, so it was offered to me to be appreciated and cataloged as a rescue.

Susan Frazier

Parent's Double Wedding Ring Quilt

I grew up seeing a double wedding ring with lavender binding on my parent's full-sized bed. Usually it was the bedspread. I would lie on it and study the little patches that made up the arced pieces attached to the solid color squares that anchored the arcs.

I had a favorite piece. It was one of tiny, tiny multi-colored polka dots. I made a game of looking for that one piece every time I was on the bed. It was machine washed and dried umpteen times from 1942 when it was a wedding present to Rosemary and Howard Grunn who raised seven kids with that quilt close by.

It was probably the impetus for my collecting the wedding ring patterned quilts I have. The family quilt disappeared for a time and was newly discovered in a plastic bag in 1995. It was worn and tattered. In 2007 I decided to restore it. I cut and patched 185 pieces to replace the worn ones. I removed the binding and replaced it in lavender. I patched a place with new batting and backing. My great grandmother would be pleased to see her gift restored and serviceable. I can only imagine all the quilts those pioneer women stitched whether for bunkhouse wall insulation or "pretties for the house."

80

Grandma's purposeful mistake

Grandma Deason's Pinwheel Star Quilt

We were married in July of 1972. One of our wedding presents was from Richard's grandmother, his mother's mother who was a cotton sharecropper from Blytheville, Arkansas. She sent us a twin-size quilt in pink and white with a calico print in the star part of the quilt. I knew nothing about quilting at the time. It was thinly batted and had a huge mistake in one of the squares. I sent grandma a thank you note and put her quilt on the linen shelf- unimpressed.

In 1975 quite a few neighborhood women gathered for brunch at Eda Smith's. As the morning wore on, we decided to form a quilting club, and each of us would make a Bicentennial quilt for 1976. I chose grandma's pinwheel star and chose white and calico blue, and calico red for my colors.

We learned the basics of layout, cutting and piecing. We met once a month and worked on our quilts. It was in one of these meetings that I learned about the mistake in grandma's quilt. It was purposeful! No one could create perfection except God.

Susan Frazier

As a result of being related to Mrs. Rose Deason, I inherited four more hand-made quilts- a sunbonnet baby, and three "string" quilts which were quilts that used scraps cut into strips to create blocks which were then sewn together in geometric designs. Nothing really special but very treasurable because of a tobacco chewin', best biscuit making old woman.

Chicken Coop Quilts

One afternoon after the holidays, I was roaming around in Lowe's when I heard my name being called. I turned and zeroed in on a "Santa like" man hailing me from across the store. I recognized him from a farmers' club I once attended. He was very excited to see me, and I soon learned that he had bought a chicken coop. (Lord, what did I care about his chicken coop?). Well, he tells me there was a wooden box in it and what do you think was in the box?

"I have no idea."

"Quilts! I thought of you because of that talk you gave the club on the quilts you find. I want you to have them. Stop by my house. I live right in town- follow me home now if you want!"

So, I show up and sure enough, in his garage is the box with five quilts in it. There were two regular blankets in there that mice had chewed and nested in which probably saved the quilts. Two quilts were pieced and knotted using pajama/ underwear fabric scraps. They were heavy and quite utilitarian. BUT the other three were crazy quilts. Sister quilts made for twin beds with very dark wool pieces and some old velvets and brocades with the signature embroidery around the piecings. There was a nondescript not-very-pretty backing too. All were terribly stinky! I took them! When I got home, I burned the blankets and stacked the quilts in the garage with their stench. Come spring, I decided no worse could be done by washing them and hanging them to dry which I did twice in cold water after first hanging them to air out for a day.

The five quilts are now quite presentable. Many thanks to Tom for thinking of me. I'd like to find a museum or some recreated semblance of pioneer life to donate them.

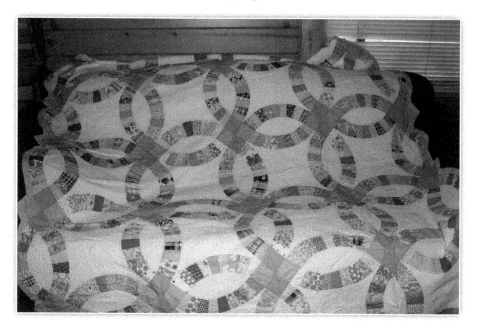

Pristine, Old but Unused New

One Summer morning on my way back from the west side of Michigan, I stopped at an antique shop just turning the open sign around. I went right to the linens arranged on several tables as if called there. In one corner was a neatly folded pastel quilt that caught my eye. As I opened it, I saw that it was a double wedding ring pattern. Looking closely, I saw the most exquisite tiny stitches. It was heavenly, handcrafted with perfection. The finishing stitches on the binding were equally tiny and perfect.

The store owner was at my elbow observing my scrutiny of the quilt. I refolded it and put it back on the table without comment and then went around the chock-full store. I appreciated the many primitive and rustic pieces; however, I went back to the quilt table a couple times more. Finally, the owner chatted with me about my interest in the aforementioned quilt. I shared my owning my parent's wedding ring quilt and thus being partial to the pattern. I commented on how new and stiff this quilt was compared to the warm, soft feel of my parent's.

"And there it is!" He said, "I know who made the quilt and where it came from. It is mid-1920s." I raised my eyebrows in surprise.

"It was made, maybe washed and folded and put on a shelf. It's been for sale here since the estate was settled. No matter where I have it in the store, it doesn't leave the store. I have an antique price on it as you can see, but I never even get an offer."

I nodded in understanding while touching the quilt again, imagining the care and joy that went into making it, but I again, walked away from the steep price. As I picked up my bag of incidental doily and handkerchief purchases, here came the owner with the quilt in his arms.

"Well, I'm not sure why I'm having such a feeling about you and this quilt, but in all the time it's been here, you have paid the most attention to it. It's called to you again and again."

He passed the quilt to my arms and said, "I'll let you have this for $25."

I squeezed it at the offer. Call it spirit, call it imagined; I was supposed to have it. It went home with me.

You know that owner could have easily washed that quilt any number of times to achieve a used condition. So, could I, but I haven't; I just admire the sewing skill of its maker, and I feel a warmth come over me.

Senior Gift Quilt

It was just after spring break for high schoolers. One of my seniors came in with a package for me all smiles. I opened it to find a patchwork quilt of blues and yellows in a cosmic design. Lauren told me that she had gone to California to visit an aunt who convinced her to try her hand at making a quilt. Guess what? The only quilt she ever makes (on spring break), and she gives it to me! Imagine that!

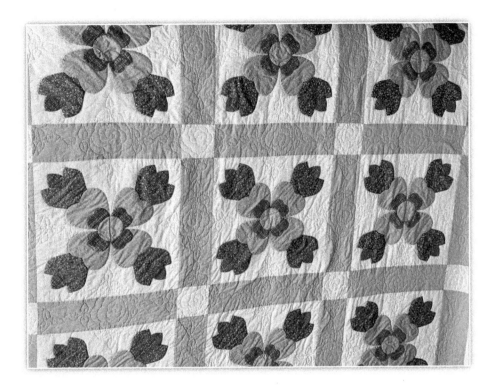

Donna's Ohio Rose

The woman who lived down the street on a dairy farm is the one who organized the neighborhood women into a quilt club. Donna was a quilt enthusiast and her first of many quilts with us was a king-sized Ohio Rose. She used it on different beds in her house after she moved from the farm. She experienced a stroke that affected her right side. She continued to piece and sew wheelchair bound. Her hand quilting changed to having quilts, mostly lap and twin size, machine quilted. One day she had me over, and it appeared she was getting her things in order to move into a nursing home. It was then that she gifted me the Ohio Rose quilt. She was an important person in my relationship with quilts. She was talented, knowledgeable, and passionate about quilting. I think about her often.

Texas Star

A friend who literally just appeared in my life recently proved to be quite a quilter whose quilting interest has waned. Robbie has a penchant for making intricate patterned quilts. She has taught numerous classes, attended tons of conferences and workshops, and worked in a quilt shop. I admire her for her expertise. We also share the loss of our veteran husbands to cancer as well as other similar experiences which make us sisters, despite our different mothers. As she was sorting and dispersing some of her stash, she found a 1930s Texas Star quilt top that she gifted me. As a result of the gift, I discovered two women who opened a machine quilting shop. I met them and found two women who retired from career jobs to do what they love- QUILT! They get to see beautiful works of many talented quilters, many vintage quilts and love every minute of it.

example of sheeting sold at cotton mills

selection of grandma's quilts

Picking Up Pieces

one of three related quilts found in the chicken coop

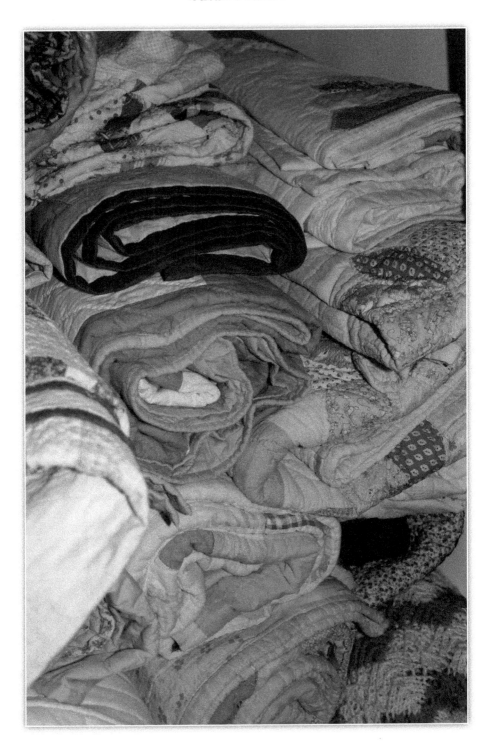

The Bedquilt

BY DOROTHY CANFIELD

O f all the Elwell family Aunt Mehetabel was certainly the most unimportant member. It was in the old time New England days, when an unmarried woman was an old maid at twenty, at forty was everyone's servant, and at sixty had gone through so much discipline that she could need no more in the next world. Aunt Mehetabel was sixty-eight.

She had never for a moment known the pleasure of being important to anyone. Not that she was useless in her brother's family; she was expected, as a matter of course, to take upon herself the most tedious and uninteresting part of the household labors. On Mondays, she accepted as her share the washing of the men's shirts, heavy with sweat and stiff with dirt from the fields and from their own hardworking bodies. Tuesdays she never dreamed of being allowed to iron anything pretty or even interesting, like the baby's white dresses or the fancy aprons of her young lady nieces. She stood all day pressing out a monotonous succession of dish-cloths and towels and sheets.

In preserving time, she was allowed to have none of the pleasant responsibility of deciding when the fruit had cooked long enough, nor did she share in the little excitement of pouring the sweet.smelling stuff into the stone jars. She sat in a corner with the children and stoned cherries incessantly, or hulled strawberries until her fingers were dyed red.

The Elwells were not consciously unkind to their aunt, they were even in a vague way fond of her; but she was so insignificant a figure in their lives that she was almost invisible to them. Aunt Mehetabel did not resent this treatment; she took it quite as unconsciously as they gave it. It was to be expected when one was an old maid dependent in a busy family. She gathered what crumbs of comfort she could from their occasional careless kindnesses and tried to hide the hurt which even yet pierced her at her brother's rough joking. In the winter when they all sat before the big hearth, roasted apples, drank mulled cider, and teased the girls about their beaux and the boys about their sweethearts, she shrank into a dusky corner with her knitting, happy if the evening passed with' out her brother saying, with a crude sarcasm, "Ask your Aunt Mehetabel about the beaux that used to come a sparkin' her!" or, "Mehetabel, how was't when you was in love with Abel Cummings?" As a matter of fact, she had been the same at twenty as at sixty, a mouselike little creature, too shy for anyone to notice, or to raise her eyes for a moment and wish for a life of her own.

Her sister-in-law, a big hearty housewife, who ruled indoors with as autocratic a sway as did her husband on the farm, was rather kind in an absent, offhand way to the shrunken little old woman, and it was through her that Mehetabel was able to enjoy the one pleasure of her life. Even as a girl she had been clever with her needle in the way of patching bedquilts. More than that she could never learn to do. The garments which she made for herself were lamentable affairs, and she was humbly grateful for any help in the bewildering business of putting them together. But in patchwork she enjoyed a tepid importance. She could really do that as well as anyone else. During years of devotion to this one art she had accumulated a considerable store of quilting patterns. Sometimes the neighbors would send over and ask "Miss Mehetabel" for the loan of her sheaf of wheat design, or the double star pattern. It was with an agreeable flutter at being able to help someone that she went to the dresser, in her bare little room under the eaves, and drew out from her crowded portfolio the pattern desired.

She never knew how her great idea came to her. Sometimes she thought she must have dreamed it, sometimes she even wondered reverently, in the phraseology of the weekly prayer meeting, if it had not been "sent" to her. She never admitted to herself that she could have thought of it without other help. It was too great, too ambitious, too lofty a project for her humble mind to have conceived.

Even when she finished drawing the design with her own fingers, she gazed at it incredulously, not daring to believe that it could indeed be her handiwork. At first it seemed to her only like a lovely but unreal dream. For a long time she did not once think of putting an actual quilt together following that pattern, even though she herself had invented it. It was not that she feared the prodigious effort that would be needed to get those tiny, oddly shaped pieces of bright-colored material sewed together with the perfection of fine workmanship needed. No, she thought zestfully and eagerly of such endless effort, her heart uplifted by her vision of the mosaic beauty of the whole creation as she saw it, when she shut her eyes to dream of it that complicated, splendidly difficult pattern good enough for the angels in heaven to quilt.

But as she dreamed, her nimble old fingers reached out longingly to turn her dream into reality. She began to think adventurously of trying it out it would perhaps not be too selfish to make one square just one unit of her design to see how it would look. She dared do nothing in the household where she was a dependent, without asking permission. With a heart full of hope and fear thumping furiously against her old ribs, she approached the mistress of the house on chuming day, knowing with the innocent guile of a child that the county woman was apt to be in a good temper while working over the flagrant butter in the cool cellar.

Sophia listened absently to her sister-in-law's halting petition. "Why, yes, Mehetabel," she said, leaning far down into the huge chum for the last golden morsels "why, yes, start another quilt if you want to. I've got a lot of pieces from the spring sewing that will work in real good." Mehetabel tried honestly to make her see that this would be no common quilt, but her limited vocabulary and her emotion stood between her and expression. At last Sophia said, with a kindly impatience: "Oh, there! Don't bother me. I never could keep track of your quiltin' patterns, anyhow. I don't care what pattern you go by."

Mehetabel rushed back up the steep attic stairs to her room, and in a joyful agitation began preparations for the work of her life. Her very first stitches showed her that it was even better than she hoped. By some heaven-sent inspiration she had invented a pattern beyond which no patchwork quilt could go.

She had but little time during the daylight hours filled with the incessant household drudgery. After dark she did not dare to sit up late at night lest she bum too much candle. It was weeks before the little square began to show the pattern. Then Mehetabel was in a fever to finish it. She was too conscientious to shirk even the smallest part of her share of the housework, but she rushed through it now so fast that she was panting as she climbed the stairs to her little room. Every time she opened the door, no matter what weather hung out. side the one small window, she always saw the little room flooded with sunshine. She smiled to herself as she bent over the innumerable scraps of cotton cloth on her work table. Already to her they were ranged in orderly, complex, mosaic beauty.

Finally she could wait no longer, and one evening ventured to bring her work down beside the fire where the family sat, hoping that good fortune would give her a place near the tallow candles on the mantelpiece. She had reached the last corner of that first square and her needle flew in and out, in and out, with nervous speed. To her relief no one noticed her. By bedtime she had only a few more stitches to add.

As she stood up with the others, the square fell from her trembling old hands and fluttered to the table. Sophia glanced at it carelessly. "Is that the new quilt you said you wanted to start?" she asked, yawning "Looks like a real pretty pattern. Let's see it."

Up to that moment Mehetabel had labored in the purest spirit of selfless adoration of an ideal. The emotional shock given her by Sophia's cry of admiration as she held the work towards the candle to examine it, was as much astonishment as joy to Mehetabel.

"Land's sakes!" cried her sister-in-law. "Why, Mehetabel Elwell, where did you git that pattern?"

"I made it up," said Mehetabel. She spoke quietly but she was trembling.

"No!" exclaimed Sophia. "Did you! Why, I never seen such a pattern in my life. Girls, come here and see what your Aunt Mehetabel is doing."

The three tall daughters turned back reluctantly from the stairs. "I never could seem to take much interest in patchwork quilts," said one. Already the old time skill born of early pioneer privation and the craving for beauty, had gone out of style.

"No, nor I neither!" answered Sophia. "But a stone image would take an interest in this pattern. Honest, Mehetabel, did you really think of it yourself?" She held it up closer to her eyes and went on, "And how under the sun and stars did you ever git your courage up to start in a making it? Land! Look at all those tiny squinchy little seams! Why, the wrong side ain't a thing but seams! Yet the good side's just like a picture, so smooth you'd think 'twas woven that way. Only nobody could."

The girls looked at it right side, wrong side, and echoed their mother's exclamations. Mr. Elwell himself came over to see what they were discussing. "Well, I declare!" he said, looking at his sister with eyes more approving than she could ever remember. "I don't know a thing about patchwork quilts, but to my eye that beats old Mis' Andrew's quilt that got the blue ribbon so many times at the County Fair."

As she lay that night in her narrow hard bed, too proud, too excited to sleep, Mehetabel's heart swelled and tears of joy ran down from her old eyes.

The next day her sister-in-law astonished her by taking the huge pan of potatoes out of her lap and setting one of the younger children to peeling them. "Don't you want to go on with that quiltin' pattern?" she said. "I'd kind o' like to see how you're goin' to make the grapevine design come out on the corner."

For the first time in her life the dependent old maid contradicted her powerful sister-in-law. Quickly and jealously she said, "It's not a grapevine. It's a sort of curlicue I made up."

"Well, it's nice looking anyhow," said Sophia pacifyingly. "I never could have made it up."

By the end of the summer the family interest had risen so high that Mehetabel was given for herself a little round table in the sitting room, for her, where she could keep her pieces and use odd minutes for her work. She almost wept over such kindness and resolved firmly not to take advantage of it. She went on faithfully with her monotonous housework, not neglecting a corner. But the atmosphere of her world was changed. Now things had a meaning. Through the longest task of washing milk pans, there rose a rainbow of promise. She took her place by the little table and put the thimble on her knotted, hard finger with the solemnity of a priestess performing a rite.

She was even able to bear with some degree of dignity the honor of having the minister and the minister's wife comment admiringly on her great project. The family felt quite proud of Aunt Mehetabel as Minister Bowman had said it was work as fine as any he had ever seen, "and he didn't know but finer!" The remark was repeated verbatim to the neighbors in the following weeks when they dropped in and examined in a perverse Vermontish silence some astonishingly difficult tour de force which Mehetabel had just finished.

The Elwells especially plumed themselves on the slow progress of the quilt. "Mehetabel has been to work on that corner for six weeks, come Tuesday, and she ain't half done yet," they explained to visitors. They fell out of the way of always expecting her to be the one to run on errands, even for the children. "Don't bother your Aunt Mehetabel," Sophia would call. "Can't you see she's got to a ticklish place on the quilt?" The old woman sat straighter in her chair, held up her head. She was a part of the world at last. She joined in the conversation and her remarks were listened to. The children were even told to mind her when she asked them to do some service for her, although this she ventured to do but seldom.

One day some people from the next town, total strangers, drove up to the Elwell house and asked if they could inspect the wonderful quilt which they had heard about even down in their end of the valley. After that, Mehetabel's quilt came little by little to be one of the local sights. No visitor in town, whether he knew the Elwells or not, went away without having been to look at it. To make her presentable to strangers, the Elwells saw to it that their aunt was better dressed than she had ever been before. One of the girls made her a pretty little cap to wear on her thin white hair.

A year went by and a quarter of the quilt was finished. A second year passed and half was done. The third year Mehetabel had pneumonia and lay ill for weeks and weeks, horrified by the idea that she might die before her work was completed. A fourth year and one could really see the grandeur of the whole design. In September of the fifth year, the entire family gathered around her to watch eagerly, as Mehetabel quilted the last stitches. The girls held it up by the four corners and they all looked at it in hushed silence.

Then Mr. Elwell cried as one speaking with authority, "By ginger! That's goin' to the County Fair!"

Mehetabel blushed a deep red. She had thought of this herself, but never would have spoken aloud of it.

"Yes indeed!" cried the family. One of the boys was dispatched to the house of a neighbor who was Chairman of the Fair Committee for their village. He came back beaming, "Of course he'll take it. Like's not it may git a prize, he says. But he's got to have it right off because all the things from our town are going tomorrow morning."

Even in her pride Mehetabel felt a pang as the bulky package was carried out of the house. As the days went on she felt lost. For years it had been her one thought. The little round stand had been heaped with litter of bright colored scraps. Now it was desolately bare. One of the neighbors who took the long journey to the Fair reported when he came back that the quilt was hung in a good place in a glass case in "Agricultural Hall." But that meant little to Mehetabel's ignorance of everything outside her brother's home. She drooped. The family noticed it. One day Sophia said kindly, "You feel sort o' lost without the quilt, don't you, Mehetabel?"

"They took it away so quick!" she said wistfully. "I hadn't hardly had one good look at it myself."

The Fair was to last a fortnight. At the beginning of the second week Mr. Elwell asked his sister how early she could get up in the morning.

"I dunno. Why?" she asked.

"Well, Thomas Ralston has got to drive to West Oldton to see a lawyer. That's four miles beyond the Fair. He says if you can git up so's to leave here at four in the morning he'll drive you to the Fair, leave you there for the day, and bring you back again at night." Mehetabel's face turned very white. Her eyes filled with tears. It was as though someone had offered her a ride in a golden chariot up to the gates of heaven. "Why, you can't mean it!" she cried wildly. Her brother laughed. He could not meet her eyes. Even to his easygoing unimaginative indifference to his sister this was a revelation of the narrowness of her life in his home. "Oh, 'tain't so much just to go to the Fair," he told her in some confusion, and then "Yes, sure I mean it. Go git your things ready, for it's tomorrow morning he wants to start."

A trembling, excited old woman stared all that night at the rafters. She who had never been more than six miles from home it was to her like going into another world. She who had never seen anything more exciting than a church supper was to see the County Fair. She had never dreamed of doing it. She could not at all imagine what it would be like.

The next morning all the family rose early to see her off. Perhaps her brother had not been the only one to be shocked by her happiness. As she tried to eat her breakfast they called out conflicting advice to her about what to see. Her brother said not to miss inspecting the stock, her nieces said the fancywork was the only thing worth looking at, Sophia told her to be sure to look at the display of preserves. Her nephews asked her to bring home an account of the trotting races.

The buggy drove up to the door, and she was helped in. The family ran to and fro with blankets, woolen tippet, a hot soapstone from the kitchen range. Her wraps were tucked about her. They all stood together and waved goodby as she drove out of the yard. She waved back, but she scarcely saw them. On her return home that evening she was ashy pale, and so stiff that her brother had to lift her out bodily. But her lips were set in a blissful smile. They crowded around her with questions until Sophia pushed them all aside. She told them Aunt Mehetabel was too tired to speak until she had had her supper. The young people held their tongues while she drank her tea, and absentmindedly ate a scrap of toast with an egg. Then the old woman was helped into an easy chair before the fire. They gathered about her, eager for news of the great world, and Sophia said, "Now, come Mehetabel, tell us all about it!"

Mehetabel drew a long breath. "It was just perfect!" she said. "Finer even than I thought. They've got it hanging up in the very middle of a sort o' closet made of glass, and one of the lower corners is ripped and turned back so's to show the seams on the wrong side."

"What?" asked Sophia, a little blankly.

"Why, the quilt!" said Mehetabel in surprise. "There are a whole lot of other ones in that room, but not one that can hold a candle to it, if I do say it who shouldn't. I heard lots of people say the same thing. You ought to have heard what the women said about that corner, Sophia. They said well, I'd be ashamed to tell you what they said. I declare if I wouldn't!"

Mr. Elwell asked, "What did you think of that big ox we've heard so much about?"

"I didn't look at the stock," returned his sister indifferently. She turned to one of her nieces. "That set of pieces you gave me, Maria, from your red waist, come out just lovely! I heard one woman say you could 'most smell the red roses."

"How did Jed Burgess' bay horse place in the mile trot?" asked Thomas.

"I didn't see the races."

"How about the preserves?" asked Sophia.

"I didn't see the preserves," said Mehetabel calmly.

Seeing that they were gazing at her with astonished faces she went on, to give them a reasonable explanation, "You see I went right to the room where the quilt was, and then I didn't want to leave it. It had been so long since I'd seen it. I had to look at it first real good myself, and then I looked at the others to see if there was any that could come up to it. Then the people begun comin' in and I got so interested in hearin' what they had to say I couldn't think of goin' anywheres else. I ate my lunch right there too, and I'm glad as can be I did, too; for what do you think?" óshe gazed about her with kindling eyes. "While I stood there with a sandwich in one hand, didn't the head of the hull concern come in and open the glass door and pin a big bow of blue ribbon right in the middle of the quilt with a label on it, 'First Prize.'"

There was a stir of proud congratulation. Then Sophia returned to questioning, "Didn't you go to see anything else?"

"Why, no," said Mehetabel. "Only the quilt. Why should I?"

She fell into a reverie. As if it hung again before her eyes she saw the glory that shone around the creation of her hand and brain. She longed to make her listeners share the golden vision with her. She struggled for words. She fumbled blindly for unknown superlatives. "I tell you it looked like" she began, and paused.

Vague recollections of hymnbook phrases came into her mind. They were the only kind of poetic expression she knew. But they were dis' missed as being sacrilegious to use for something in real life. Also as not being nearly striking enough.

Finally, "I tell you it looked real good," she assured them and sat staring into the fire, on her tired old face the supreme content of an artist who has realized his ideal.

CPSIA information can be obtained
at www.ICGtesting.com
Printed in the USA
LVHW011146211121
703954LV00005B/90